There were more than fifty people working around the excavation. Beyond the harsh brilliance of the arc lights the alien stars shone jewel-bright, jewel-hard out of the polar night.

Occasionally one of them broke the pattern of their coming and going to claw loose some promisingly hard lump from the frozen soil, crumble it, examine it, and throw it aside.

This was Regis, the loneliest outpost of the human race, further from Earth than any other planet men had visited. On this planet, artifacts had been found ... they had not been made by humans.

On the planet Regis, now, this little group of excavators were about to discover the final evidence that there were really *others* in the universe, that they had visited Regis in the recent past — and that they would return. ...

"Very enjoyable, very competent."

— Frederik Pohl, *IF SCIENCE FICTION*

P

on us for help

THE WORLD SWAPPERS

JOHN BRUNNER writes of himself:

"Biographical data? Born, I believe; Married, 12th July 1958; dead, not yet. I've been reading science-fiction since I was seven and writing it since I was nine — but I didn't actually collect my first rejection slip till I was 13 ...

"I don't regard myself in any sense as a quote creative writer unquote. I prefer to communicate with my audience, not make them puzzled, and consequently am not all that fond of literary obscurities such as typify modern, recognized, *literature*.

"Out of sympathy with: intolerance of all kinds, the beat generation, angry young men, and angry old women. In sympathy with: the human race — it's in a hell of a mess."

Other ACE BOOKS by John Brunner:

THE WORLD SWAPPERS

by

JOHN BRUNNER

ace books

A Division of Charter Communications Inc.

1120 Avenue of the Americas

New York, N.Y. 10036

An ACE Book

CHAPTER I

COUNCE launched the end of his cigarette into the air with a gentle flick of his fingers. It soared out over the side of the boat and extinguished itself with the faintest of hisses in the green water of mid-Pacific. Otherwise he did not move.

He was half-sitting, half-lying, with his back against the hard, sun-warmed cover of the propulsor. One excessively long leg was stretched out along the fender which rimmed the gunwale, barely sinking into the resilient plastic; the other dangled over the reactor well.

A gull which had been circling down to look him over, and which had almost decided he was not worth paying attention to, saw the white object arc overboard, swooped, and neatly lifted the disintegrating butt out of the sea. At once it dropped the sour-tasting thing again with a mewing cry of dismay, gave Counce a hurt look, and flapped off with injured dignity. Counce followed its movements idly for a few yards.

Then his face suddenly lost all traces of awareness, as if he had cut himself off from the present. For a while he remained quite still, seeming to listen, before his right hand shot out and twitched the helm and accelerator levers

1

together. The boat described a quarter turn and came to rest again, rocking slightly in its own ripples, the steam from the propulsor hanging around the stern like a patch of localized fog. The blind panes of Counce's dark glasses turned towards the blue horizon, facing the one point where no one else would have expected to see anything. No one else, that is, except someone who had come to this precise place for this precise reason.

Behind him now, though very far away, the tentacles of the purification and extraction plants spread yearly further southward; to his right, somewhat nearer, were the kelp farms of Pacific Nutrition; to his left and nearer again, though still below the skyline, was the smart and somewhat snobbish residential district of Sealand. In the direction in which Counce faced, there was nothing for a thousand miles bar a few scattered islands.

Then there was a gleam as if Venus had become visible in the middle of the day and too far from the plane of the ecliptic. It was very faint, and the sun competed with it, but the dark glasses helped, and the distance was closing rapidly — at about twelve hundred miles an hour, he judged.

The gleam took on form by degrees. The hull showed first, as a darker blob; then the wings, their leading edges glowing sullen red; and last of all the thin lines of the hydrofins. Counce nodded approval as the spaceship slanted down toward the water. The pilot knew his job — he, Counce, could hardly have chosen the angle of approach better himself.

The first hydrofin bit the water, and the rate of increase of the ship's apparent size dropped abruptly. It was still more than twenty miles away, but a vessel capable of carrying a crew of a dozen on hundred-parsec hops could not very well be inconspicuously small.

The spray from the second layer of hydrofins turned to

steam as they touched and briefly left the water again; with a cry of tortured metal the hot wings were suddenly struck and chilled. The ship skimmed over the ocean, settling slowly to its normal riding attitude as it bore down on Counce's boat. It threw out first a sea anchor, then, when its detectors had checked the bottom profile, a tractor beam focused on the crest of the nearest submarine peak. It came to a halt less than a half mile away.

And disappeared.

Counce sighed, taking off his dark glasses and putting them away in the pouch of his trunks. The deck of the boat was heating up under him, which meant that someone aboard the spaceship had put two and two together in an unusually inspired manner. Had Bassett somehow been warned about him? Counce thought it unlikely, but he would have to make allowances for the possibility.

He gathered himself in a single movement and tossed himself languidly after the cigarette just as the sonic found the critical resonance of the metal hull and the boat shivered into steaming fragments. Immediately the heavy weight of the shielded propulsor dropped towards the floor of the ocean, its automatic capsize guards going up with a succession of sharp clicking noises. In this much water, it would hardly be worth salvaging.

Feeling the brief wave of warmth from the shattered boat wash about his body, Counce trod water and stared at the place where the spaceship had been. Even with the guards up, the propulsor would have shed enough radioactivity in the immediate vicinity to fog the detectors for a while, so he was at liberty to go about the task of superoxygenating his bloodstream with deep breaths before he needed to duck. They would, he supposed, have shielded the underside of the ship as well as the superstructure in case one of the local fishguards in his submersible spotted it and remembered. However, from underneath was the logical mode of approach — he couldn't fly.

Dodging a shoal of frightened fish bearing the Dateline Fisheries brand on their dorsal fins, Counce began to swim towards the point at which the ship had vanished. He reached the edge of the barrier sooner than he had expected, and trod water again as he felt the tingling of the blanking frequencies greet his outstretched fingertips. They'd set it for maximum output, then — they weren't taking any chances. Except, naturally, the ones they didn't know about.

He made a swift calculation. He had been under for six minutes three seconds already, and the additional six minutes or so which it would take him to negotiate the barrier would bring him perilously close to his safety margin. He would have surfaced if he could, but the problem of navigating through these screens partly in a liquid and partly in gas added unnecessary complications to the job. From below was not just the logical way — it was the only way.

He swung his mental compass, closed his eyes, and deliberately committed himself to his own personal inertial guidance system. He forced himself to disregard all sensory impressions except the changing pressure of water on his skin and the position of the fluid in his semicircular canals, telling him which way was up. Gravity was the one thing he could expect to remain constant within the barrier; the ship was on Earth, and Counce knew perfectly well that for the time being it was meant to remain here, so that at least they would not be monkeying with the value of g. But if he deviated from the straight path he was going to be in trouble.

Exactly six minutes later he surfaced and opened his eyes to the greenish light which was all that soaked past the barrier — the light from *below* the surface, not from above. He found two men looking at him. That implied that Bassett did not have implicit faith in his excellent defenses, and that in turn suggested he had heard about Counce after all. Counce trod water, waiting to die.

The men who stood on the wing of the spaceship regarded him curiously while he replenished his lungs. The one on the left had a gun leveled at Counce's chest — not at the point where his chest appeared to be; this man knew all about refraction. The other one, Counce presumed, would be Bassett. Interesting.

Finally, the one he took to be Bassett gestured to his companion, and the latter lowered his gun. Counce felt a surge of relief. It was pretty much an axiom that little is to be feared from a man who comes naked and unarmed, but Bassett had got where he was by disregarding axioms like that.

"All right, you," said the man with the gun. "Come aboard." He kicked the catch of the disembarkation ladder, and hiduminium legs plopped into the water a few yards from Counce. Acting rather more fatigued than he in fact was, he swam to the ladder and hauled himself up, dripping. He looked about him at the ship and found it much as he had expected; the distinctive shape of the bulge aft of the control blister implied a Metchnikov drive, which shouldn't strictly speaking have been fitted to a private vessel, but Bassett had the key to many unlikely storerooms.

"Get this guy a towel, Lecoq!" shouted the man with the gun, and in a moment someone tossed one through the open door of the airlock. Counce's hand was waiting for it when it arrived; the significance of this fact was lost on the two men watching. He rubbed himself quickly down, but he was still leaving wet footprints when they judged the job had taken long enough and urged him inside.

The curious eyes of the man at the detector panel followed him as he went down a narrow passage and into a room located amidships. Two of the original cabins must have been knocked into one to make this sizable compartment, Counce judged, and immediately wondered if the crew knew what the removal of a bulkhead did to the stress system of a ship entering hyperspace. Apparently they did; a second glance revealed little gray nodules welded along the line of the missing partition — the visible ends of a dozen compensators.

"Sit down," said Bassett from behind him, and the door closed.

Counce obeyed, and his unwilling host came around in front of him and sat down on the other side of a transparent table in the depths of which was sunk a game of three-dimensional chess. The pieces were set for a mate for white in nine.

He looked directly at the other, seeing a tall, thin sandy-haired man, his face lean; with deep-set gray eyes, his hands strong and short-fingered. With the kind of geriatric treatment such a man could afford, Bassett could have been anywhere between forty and a hundred; Counce knew he was in fact near the lower, not the upper end of the scale.

Sitting back relaxedly, he capitalized on Bassett's discomfort by allowing him to take the initiative. The silence stretched elastically as Bassett looked the intruder up and down and confirmed that he did not look unlike an ordinary man.

At length he said, "Well, what do you want?"

Counce found the choice of question illuminating. Bassett might have been expected to say, "Who are you?" But Counce did not react perceptibly; he merely answered,

"I think it would perhaps be better if I told you first that I already know what *you* want."

Bassett's face betrayed a slight puzzlement. "All right," he agreed. "Tell me what I want."

"You want to rule the galaxy," said Counce.

CHAPTER II

THE GALAXY

As good a name for it as any, for people who had barely gotten used to thinking of their back yard as a part of Earth before they had to adjust to the idea of Earth as one planet of a solar system, and then to the system being just one corner of the universe. Vocabulary had lagged behind facts ever since the first tide of real achievement had swamped mankind.

The galaxy, then, though strictly only a very small part of it. Specifically, the thirty-one planets within a radius of two hundred parsecs or so which had been populated by man: thinly, true — ten million here, a hundred million on some of the older worlds — but populated.

The galaxy, human version: a relatively narrow segment of the cartwheel of stars centered on Sagittarius, but wide enough. Wide enough to have accepted people by the cityful when the drivers were first developed, to have offered escape to people who were frightened, unsettled, hungry, idealistic — who needed to get the hell out. That had acted as a safety valve.

Now the boiler was beginning to strain again.

This, then, was Earth in the twenty-sixth century: fat,

sleek, well-fed, though forced to adopt devious means to achieve that end; feeling the faintest, ghostliest hint of discomfort, wondering at last whether it had not only never had it so good, but whether it was ever going to have it so good again.

Three and four centuries before, men of Earth had gone by the hundreds of thousands to seek their new worlds. They had found them, and ceased to be men *of Earth*. Naturally. That was why Bassett was here. That was why Counce had been waiting for him.

Bassett was taken aback, and, to cover himself while he thought over Counce's challenging remark, he opened a box which rested on the transparent tabletop. It was a memento of the visit he had just made; even if he had not known where Bassett had been, Counce could have guessed that the box was made on Boreas. For one thing, it was ornamented with silver, and only a poor colonial world could afford to waste high-conductivity metals on knick-knacks. The box held slim brown cigarillos; he accepted one.

"Thanks," he said wryly. "My cigarettes were soaked when you sank my boat so expertly."

Bassett ignored the remark, closed the box after taking a cigarillo for himself; and passed an igniter across the table. "You're possessed of unusual physical abilities," he mused. "I'd have assumed you also had peculiar powers of intelligence if you hadn't made such an empty-sounding remark. Suppose I ask what you intended it to mean?"

"Let me say also that I know why you have just visited Boreas," Counce answered obliquely, and Bassett frowned.

"My company does a large off-world trade in luxury trinkets," he prevaricated. "I've been to a number of the worlds where we have contacts — "

"But never previously to renew a contract which has been losing you profit steadily for more than a year," Counce interrupted. "Suppose we stop fencing. Let's look at it this way. In the normal course of events, you, being a very able man, could expect to be on top of the heap here on Earth in another forty years' time. You'd still be young enough to enjoy several years of power. But you're impatient, so it's doubtful whether the prospect would have satisfied you anyway. However, the question scarcely arises any more, because you learned some time back that forty or fifty years from now Earth will most likely be passing through a severe crisis. On the most generous permissible estimates, the population curve is going to cut the standard of living curve and chop it off. People are going to be dissatisfied, unsettled; they'll look for places to go, and there won't be any unless someone provides them.

"Out there are thirty-one habitable and sparsely populated worlds. Practically without exception, they hate the guts of Earth, because their founding fathers expected Earth to get bogged down in its own population density and sink towards poverty, while they, the colonials, rose to unheard-of heights. Take Ymir, for example. The pioneers went out there in a rush of righteous indignation, parked themselves on the first lump of mud with breathable air that they chanced upon, neglecting the fact that it was in the middle of a glacial period, and kept themselves warm by fanning this indignation of theirs to maximum temperature.

"But that was three hundred years ago, and the flames are dying down. The Ymirans can't admit to themselves that their ancestors were fools to pass up their chance of a share in the peace and comfort of twenty-sixth century

Earth; yet below the surface they envy us so much they're *sick*. They doubtless have plenty of natural resources — only most of them are under two hundred feet of solid ice.

"There are misfits and malcontents here on Earth even now. When the squeeze comes in another few decades, some people are going to look around for an escape. And it will make no difference that nowadays, with the Metchnikov drive, you could put the whole population of Rio or Greater Tokyo aloft in a single ship. You'd run up against the square-cube law: within the radius of explored space there are no habitable virgin worlds for people to go to.

"The obvious answer is to re-open the colonial worlds already planted to a fresh wave of Earthborn. And that's what you propose to do; you're intending to buy the good will of the colonial planets with technical and other assistance, so that when the time comes you'll be the man who can offer the way of escape people are looking for.

"But there will be conflict. Your computers predict that, and they're right. The newcomers will struggle with the colonists; because the newcomers will have the pioneering urge, and the colonists are disillusioned, the newcomers will win — and they'll owe their greatest loyalty to you."

Counce finished his long speech in the same level tone he had used throughout, and looked at Bassett, wondering what his reaction would be. It took a long time coming, but it was a tacit admission. That was another reason why Bassett was on his way to the top: he wasted no time on things like useless denials.

He said, "In outline, that's correct. I don't pretend to guess how you know, but if that's your motive for saying I want to rule the galaxy, you're wrong, of course. You can't *rule* the galaxy."

"That's so true it's a platitude," agreed Counce.

"However, we needn't quibble about what 'ruling' actually consists of."

Bassett nodded. "But I still want to know why you came."

"I came to tell you that your mission to Boreas was a complete waste of time. In view of the fact that Boreas is one of the few outworlds that is kindly disposed towards Earth, you jumped to the obvious — but wrong — conclusion that it was the best place to start buying your good will for the future. Your computers will tell you that, but if I hadn't come to see you, you'd have assumed insufficient data was the trouble, and maybe you'd have spent another ten months or a year hammering away at the problem before giving up. You might even have been discouraged enough to go back to a problem which is genuinely insoluble — how to avert Earth's coming crisis."

"Now look here," said Bassett, "we ourselves haven't had a chance to evaluate our findings yet. You, and whoever else is behind you, can't conceivably have had an advance report. To start with, this is one of the fastest civil ships in space, and I doubt whether anyone in your group, whoever they may be, has access to a Metchnikov driver."

"True," conceded Counce, not mentioning that they got along excellently without needing Metchnikov drivers.

The implied tribute to his deductive ability touched Bassett's perfectly human vanity. He said, "You know, I've heard stories from time to time, which seemed incredible but made me keep my eyes open. You might say, I guess, that I'd been watching out for you."

"Whereas I was *waiting* for you," Counce reminded him. He drew the knife of his words deep, and gave the wound a chance to fester in Bassett's self-esteem before continuing.

12

"Your greatest difficulty is that you don't know what your problem really is."

"Indeed!" snapped Bassett. "And by what right do you claim to know better than I?"

"Suppose we say," Counce murmured, "that my friends and I have studied the matter for a longer time than you have. But that's beside the point. I'm going to tell you straight out that the solution to the problem is not to be found on Boreas, but on Ymir. Having done that, I'll give you two alternatives. You can decide that you want me to tackle the Ymiran problem for you and bring you the answer, in which case you can buy time on the Falconetta program over Video India — no special message, it'll be conspicuous enough. I know you never patronize the show with your advertising; you don't like the limits Ram Singh puts on the use of hypnotics. Word will get to me. Alternatively, you can turn me over the side and forget about me."

He raised a hand to forestall a question budding on Bassett's lips. "There isn't a third alternative," he said. "You won't crack the Ymiran problem by yourself. It'll be tough for me, and I'm a specialist in problems."

"You're good at settling them, certainly," acknowledged Bassett. "But I'm not totally unpracticed myself, of course. I presume your mind is very well armored indeed, or you'd never have ventured here alone. That implies there's no quick way I could dig the knowledge you claim to possess out of your mind. But I'm patient enough to resort to a long, slow way if I have to."

The threat wasn't even a veiled one. Counce got to his feet and stared down at the other across the transparent table. "I said there was no third choice, Bassett," he snapped. "Check your detector board. There's a Dateline Fisheries sub cruising in a tight circle round the limits of your barrier. Bear in mind that a genuine fishguard's sub wouldn't know there was a ship here. You'd be well advised to let me swim out to it."

"Is that true?" Bassett asked the air; well, it was only to be expected that he'd have eavesdroppers on such an important conversation.

"Yes," answered a voice from the ceiling. "But what the hell could a sub do to us behind our screens? Suppose we jump a couple of miles!"

"I shouldn't," said Counce, a hint of amusement edging his tone.

According to their psych-profile of him, Bassett ought to have been sufficiently fuddled by the strangeness of Counce's arrival to have failed to see the obvious: that there was nothing a sub could do to them behind so much screening. Counce could feel the tension mounting inside him.

"I think you've been rather stupid," said Basset at last. "Yes, Lecoq, by all means jump a couple of miles."

Counce sighed, and stubbed his cigarillo.

"And send a couple of men in here," Bassett ordered.

They entered; they were large and muscular and determined, and when Bassett nodded at Counce they closed in, intending to take him prisoner. Apologetically Counce struck each of them under the jaw with enough force to render them unconscious; he hit the one on the left with slightly too much violence, and blood dribbled from the site of a tooth as the man fell.

"Lecoq!" shouted Bassett, leaping to his feet.

"I'm putting the ship in orbit," said the voice from the ceiling. "I daren't turn loose a gun in there!"

Trembling all over, Bassett backed as far away from Counce as he could — about four feet.

"I told you there was no third alternative," said Counce

14

again, sharply this time, managing to convey that he felt he was dealing with a backward child.

And in his turn, he disappeared.

CHAPTER III

THERE WERE more than fifty people working around the excavation, and yet never in his young life had Anty Dreean felt so completely alone. Beyond the harsh brilliance of the arc lights the alien stars of Regis sky shone jewel-bright jewel-hard, out of the polar night. His breath, and that of all the other men and women present, misted whitely as they exhaled; they clapped their hands and stamped their feet in spite of the encumbering parkas and fur breeches they wore.

He stood at the control panel of the lighting system, alert to answer any calls for increased brilliance in the pit before him. This pit was a hundred feet long and perhaps twenty feet wide at its widest. Moving methodically along its floor, carrying sensitive detection instruments, were half a dozen men and women. Occasionally they broke the pattern of their coming and going to claw loose some promisingly hard lump from the frozen soil, crumble it, examine the result, and throw it aside before resuming their task.

An intruder might have guessed at an archeological survey in progress. The guess would have been more than half wrong. For this was Regis, loneliest outpost of the human race, further from Earth than any other planet men had ever visited, and people had come here so lately and in such small numbers that nothing extracted from the ground would have said anything significant about their doings.

Yet the guess would have been at least partly right, too. The technique was similar to archeological excavation; the painstaking thoroughness was identical. But the searchers were not after anything as neutral as knowledge for its own sake — they were desperately seeking a warning of danger. A danger that might be the greatest the human race had ever faced.

In spite of his awareness of the consequences, Anty Dreean found himself wishing that the waiting might end and that they might find the certainty they feared.

At the end of the pit nearest to where Anty stood, Wu, the director of the expedition on Regis, and his senior aide, Katya Ivanovna, moved like grotesque, oversized dolls. In Wu's hands was a sonar detector; its staring telltale eye flickered and changed as its beam recorded the presence of solid matter in the walls of the pit, and Katya dug at it with a trowel. Anty leaned forward, wondering if this was going to be it.

Abruptly, he was recalled to his task by a charp command — the voice had probably been Lotus Scharf's. He stepped up the level of illumination at the opposite end of the pit, and people all around, as though moved by a premonition, hesitated and turned to see what had happened.

Something glittered in Lotus' gauntleted hands. She beckoned urgently to Wu, who hurried across to her. For a few moments their hooded heads were bent together as they conferred.

From the rim of the excavation someone uttered the

question which had been burning for long moments in Anty's own mind; he strained forward to hear the answer.

A little stiffly, a little solemnly, Wu raised his head and spoke. "It's a food container," he said. "An empty can — and it's not one of ours."

So the Others *had* been to Regis. And that meant they might come back.

The gathering began to break up; someone went over to the transfax and started it, so that the leakage of light from its tremendous field of pent-up power made the landscape like day. Wu handed his sonar detector over the edge of the pit, and scrambled up after it, as did the rest of the workers. Only Anty Dreean seemed to be frozen to immobility.

In the few seconds it took for Wu and his companions to leave the pit, Anty found time to review the whole series of events that had climaxed here, now, on the permafrozen tundra of Regis' north pole. It had begun a very long way away, on Wu's home world of K'ung-fu-tse, when a laboratory worker engaged in measuring certain atomic resonance frequencies had found his results to be disturbed by vibrations in the very fabric of space.

There were thousands of sets of vibrations such as these now, spreading through the galaxy like the wake of so many ships. That was exactly what they were — the wake of ships, driven faster than light, and straining the framework of the universe. They could be ignored, of course; they produced no noticeable effects on anything at a distance greater than a few thousand miles. Except when it came to such delicate operations as studying the interior of atomic nuclei.

There was a standard technique for dealing with the problem, tedious, but adequate, which consisted of determining the source of the vibrations to a high degree of accuracy and then calculating what allowance to make for their influence. Swearing, the laboratory worker proceeded to apply the method — and found that the source was in the wrong place.

It lay out towards Regis. And because he happened — by a minor miracle — to be a friend of Wu's and party to a good many secrets which most people did not share, the worker felt the hairs rise on the back of his neck.

There should not have been any vibrations of this kind in the neighborhood of Regis. No human-built ship had ever been to Regis. Men had visited the planet, true, but they had traveled by a different route.

So he had shouted a warning.

They had known for a very long time that the laws of chance alone insisted that man was not unique in the cosmos; somewhere there must be other creatures with an urge towards the stars and the technical ability to fulfill that urge. For a shorter time, they had known what the nearest non-human space-going species was, and where it held sway. That was why men had come to Regis, a world ideally situated as a base from which to keep an eye on their potential competitors.

But now — !

The Others had been to Regis already. What if they were to come back? Much of this world's surface was temperate and therefore too warm for their comfort; here at the pole the climate was quite suitable, though — and even if the prevailing planetary average made it unlikely they would decide to plant a colony here, there was always a risk. Look at what men had done on Ymir, that icebox of a world!

Anty felt a chill that was not all due to his environment.

Slowly, he returned to the reality around him, and heard his name being called. They had cut off the power from the floodlights, and were now working by the leakage from the transfax field; its glare shifted irregularly from white to green and back, and when it was in the green phase everything looked ghastly. Someone was waving to him from beside the transfax platform. Katya.

Dutifully, but despondently, Anty answered the call.

"Anty, I hate doing this to you," Katya said as he came within earshot. "Only there doesn't seem to be much choice. I'm going to ask you to stay behind here for a bit longer and see what else you can turn up that the Others left behind. We've got some really high-pressure planning to do."

"And you can get on with it better if I'm not in the way," Anty said with acid sarcasm. "What do you want the rest of that garbage for? Isn't simple proof enough for you?"

Katya's broad Slavonic face reflected momentary indecision; then she put one enormously bulky arm companionably around Anty's shoulders. "Anty, honey, I know how you feel, believe me. But what can we do about it except our best? We aren't trying to shuffle you off out of the way; it's just that we need every scrap of information we can get out of this hole here. How big the visitors' expedition was; how it was equipped — get me?"

Anty took a deep breath and mastered himself. "I'm sorry, Katya. It's — well, it's everything put together, I guess. Being the newest recruit here on Regis, and being practically the only non-Earthborn person —"

Katya made to say something, but Anty rushed on. "Yes, I know what you're going to say. All of us have to go through the experience of being Johnny-come-lately, and there are so many more people on Earth than on all the other worlds put together that it's only natural for me to be on my own, and that with my lack of experience I can be more valuable doing the dirty work than helping to draft policy — I *know*, blast it! I simply can't make myself compute with it all the time."

Katya gave him a broad grin. "You've won half your battle already, Anty. It takes some people an awfully long time to learn to make frank admissions like that one! But there's another thing you ought to get through your head, and if you get that straight as well, you'll be fully equipped."

Anty nodded, his eyes on Katya's face.

"The human mind, Anty — and remember, 'human' includes you — just isn't fitted to live with the certainty of impending disaster twenty-four hours a day. You have to have some sort of relief, or you'll break down. Laugh! Sing! Let yourself go!"

"Laugh?" echoed Anty sourly. "What at?"

"Look for something. The expression on Counce's face, for example — can't you picture him when he hears that his carefully worked out plans for handling Bassett will have to be chopped to pieces?"

"You call that funny? I'd have said it was a shame!"

Katya shrugged. "It's part of the universe-as-it-is. To give you a clearer example: half an hour ago we didn't know that the Others had been to Regis. We know now. You're thinking of it as a disaster. But damnation, it isn't! The disaster would have been if we *hadn't* found out; the actual discovery is a relief."

Anty turned it over in his mind, and at length gave a reluctant nod. Katya clapped him on the back approvingly.

"Lotus is staying here for the time being too," she said. "We'd spare more people if we could, because we desperately need to find out what's down that hole. But we can't, so it's up to you and her."

Again Anty nodded, and with a parting smile Katya

turned and climbed through the transfax back to Main Base.

Practically everything else had gone by now; all the time he had been talking with Katya the others had been manhandling the equipment up the ramp to the transfax platform, and he was startled to see that there was now nothing left except two shovels, one large floodlight, and Lotus herself. She was offering him one of the shovels.

"Shall we get busy?" she suggested in her dry, precise voice. "The quicker we get started, the quicker we can get the hell out."

Anty nodded, accepted the shovel, and jumped down into the pit. Digging! Actually pushing this hard ground aside with his own strength! He might as well have stayed home on Boreas and lived a nice comfortable life without knowing about the transfax, and the existence of the Others, and the hundred and one other uncomfortable secrets to which he had been initiated since he'd come to Regis.

The transfax went off, and night returned to the area. Glancing about him, Anty was struck by the sterile ugliness of the scene. Yet to the alien visitors who had come here the landscape would not have been repulsive; to them, this bare ground layered with frost and patched with snowdrifts would have been familiar — perhaps beautiful.

He tried to imagine the view through alien eyes. There would have been their ship; they would have scouted the planet and found it uninhabited except by the blobs of primal protoplasm in its soupy seas; then, secure, they would have chosen the most comfortable spot for a landing, camped here, and gone about their business.

When they were done, they would have buried their garbage and sterilized the local soil for fear of contaminating it with their own symbiotic microorganisms.

And they would have gone away. Perhaps they would never return. There were more worlds that men had considered and discarded than there were worlds where they had planted colonies.

His shovel chinked against something, and he turned out the first alien artifact he had ever held in his own hands. Awe filled him as he picked it up and looked at it. It was no more than a broken cathode-ray tube, shattered perhaps by careless handling. But it had been conceived in an alien mind, and that was what counted.

Anty's misery evaporated like frost in sunlight. This useless piece of scrap he held was recognizable, but it was *different*. How to communicate the excitement that difference inspired in him? There was the problem in a nutshell: how to make people find differences like this exciting, and not frightening. It *could* be done, couldn't it? It would *have* to be done.

CHAPTER IV

THE INTERIOR of the submersible — which was in fact a perfectly ordinary fishguard's craft belonging to Dateline Fisheries and unofficially borrowed for the occasion — was very crowded. Half the available space was taken up by the transfax platform; the robot mechanic supervising its operation blocked off access to the dolphin kennel, and the rest of the cabin was nearly completely filled by Ram Singh and his flowing white beard, and by Falconetta, looking as usual quite dishearteningly beautiful.

When Counce arrived, therefore, he perforce remained on the transfax platform. At first he said nothing. There was no sound except the burr of the propulsor and the hum of the ventilation fans as they dealt with the heat generated by operating the transfax field.

During the pregnant silence, he removed from the belt of his shorts the neatly packaged video-audio unit which had kept the others apprised of his doings. It consisted of a flexible strip of plastic covered with printed circuitry and ostensibly decorated with twin multifaceted bosses on either side of the fastening. Bassett had dismissed it without a second thought. That was about the only thing that had gone exactly according to plan.

Weighing the unit meditatively in his hand, Counce lowered his body to a squatting position and said, "Some time, Ram, we are going to *have* to figure what's missing from a psych-profile. Didn't you assure me Bassett would be confused enough by the circumstances of my arrival to let me go and ask no questions?"

Ram bent his noble head as if to avoid Counce's gaze. "There's always one unpredictable factor — how the individual will react to your actual physical presence. I'm sorry if you consider that I failed you, Saïd. Meantime, though, I think we should be gone from here before Bassett returns; he sent his ship into orbit at about six hundred miles, and it will not take him long to land again."

Stiffly, the old man turned to the pilot desk, and lost himself in the careful maneuvering of the vessel. Counce threw the belt over a nearby hook and sat back against the wall.

"I think that was hardly kind of you," said Falconetta, passing her right hand through her long black hair. The tresses rustled on the gold lamé of her sari. Counce gave a shrug.

"I agree. Sorry. I just don't feel in a mood to apologize right now. After all, we were relying on Ram —"

"Exactly. If anybody in the galaxy could have prepared a workable plan, it was Ram. That his idea didn't come off merely shows that we've all been at fault in underestimating Bassett. It doesn't detract from Ram's ability." She turned her smoky-yellow eyes speculatively in the direction of the pilot desk. "He knows so damned much about applied psychology, I sometimes wonder why he isn't dictator of Earth instead of producer of a video show."

"You know quite well why he's not. Like ninety-nine per cent of the susceptible males on Earth, he's hopelessly in love with you, and he wouldn't settle for being dictator of Earth if he couldn't dictate to you too. Which he couldn't."

"I suppose you're right," said Falconetta with a trace of weariness. "But I've gotten so used to making people fall for me that it's a positive relief to be with you, Saïd. I know you don't give a damn one way or the other."

"Hello, human being," said Counce, and quirked his lips.

"Human yourself," said Falconetta with a fleeting smile. "Seriously, though, Saïd — I know I don't have any say in the matter, but I think it might be as well for me to be ugly next time, if you follow me." She looked down approvingly at her slender, graceful body, and shook her head. "I shall miss this . . . but I'm desperately afraid of coming to rely too much on physical attractiveness and not enough on my own ability."

"I don't think there's much risk of that. But I'll try and drop a hint. Were you beautiful before?"

"Not as beautiful as I am now. I turned a few heads. But when I found myself like this, it was a — a shock, you know?"

Counce nodded. "It's always a shock. It's always different. But adapting to the difference is like riding a bicycle or swimming — once you've learned, the talent of adjustment stays with you. I should know."

Falconetta nodded. "How many times have you died, Saïd? I don't think I've ever asked."

"Five." Counce's eyes seemed for a moment to lose their focus, as if he was staring into memory. "The first time is always the worst."

Falconetta shuddered. "I hope so. Did you ever go back and look at yourself?"

"No. Did you?" Counce regarded her curiously; she gave a slow nod.

"It was back on Shiva, where I was born. I went and looked at the headstone on my own grave. But the thought that there was the name I had called my own, and the idea that under that stone was the flesh I had lived inside of — ugh! I shall never do it again."

Ram finished setting the course on the pilot desk; now he turned the chair to face the others, and Counce made a small movement that accepted him into the discussion.

"Where precisely did we go wrong?" Ram inquired. "We followed you on the screen, of course, but there's certain information — atmosphere, if you like — which doesn't come through."

Counce spread his hands helplessly. "Mainly, I think we failed to realize just what an intelligent man Bassett is. And by intelligent, I mean adjusted to facts as they present themselves. His selective inattention level must be incredibly low."

"I wish we could give him the facts," Falconetta said musingly. "He is the sort of man we need."

"Not quite. If intelligence were enough, we could appeal to him — intelligence is logical, after all. It's pride and self-esteem that present the difficulties, and Bassett has plenty of those." Counce punched fist into palm. "We need him and what he can do for us. He needs us too, though he doesn't know what for, wouldn't admit it if he did — and in any case we can't tell him. Paradoxical, isn't it?"

Ram exhaled with a gusty sigh. "Yes," he said: "Like most very intelligent men, he is expert at looking after himself. Which implies that you and I would not rate very high on any scale of practical intelligence."

"Because we spend a stupidly large amount of time worrying about other people?" Falconetta suggested.

"Exactly. Check the school records over the centuries — the infant geniuses have gone on to become business giants and administrators, not social reformers, artists, poets. Intelligence manifested as common sense."

"Not quite," objected Counce. "Common sense ought to prevent Bassett from doing as he intends to do. If his plans materialized, the thing that would please him most would be that he was the man who opened up the outworlds, who made the outworlds other Earths. And that's the most dangerous fiction of all, because they *aren't!* An outworlder is a human being, but he's not an Earthman, and Bassett would treat him as if he were. You can't reduce millions of unique individuals to a single common pattern; if they're all being made to behave according to a norm, most of them are being driven to act in ways more or less foreign to their nature. Can you imagine people on Boreas, Astraea, Ymir, everywhere, all being hammered into a mold meant for Earthmen? That's what Bassett would do, and the results would be terrifying!"

Falconetta shuddered. "I know. And yet he isn't what you'd call an evil man."

"No. Just inexperienced."

The robot operating the transfax gave them a polite warning, and the cabin filled with a flash of brilliant light as something materialized on the platform. Frowning, Counce picked it up — a single sheet of paper with a brief message on it. He scanned it, and then deliberately folded it up before looking at the others.

"What's the most disastrous thing you can conceive happening in the immediate future?" he asked.

"Bassett ignoring our intrusion?" suggested Falconetta with a frown. "After all, he now knows there's someone in the galaxy with a workable matter transmitter, which is the worst mistake we've made in years. What that may do to his thinking —"

"Bad," conceded Counce. "But not the worst. We could always assassinate him if we were driven to it. Ram?"

"Discovery of Ymir by the Others," the old man said,

and Counce nodded emphatically.

"Very bad indeed. You've more or less bracketed what has actually happened. This note is from Wu on Regis — the Others visited it before we got there. They've dug up proof."

Their faces reflected their dismay. "That's awful," whispered Falconetta. "And coming on top of what Bassett did . . ."

"You already have an idea," said Ram, scrutinizing Counce's face keenly. "Saïd, you have one of the keenest minds in the galaxy; let us hear what your suggestion is."

"Well, this makes it absolutely essential for us to make Bassett lose patience with his own ability to solve the Ymiran problem. Could you imagine him refusing to jump at a real live Ymiran, right here on Earth?"

"There *are* Ymirans on Earth," objected Falconetta. "They have an embassy in Rio about four blocks from Bassett's head office."

"But they staff the place with the least corruptible and most masochistic of the faithful. Since Jaroslav, there hasn't been anyone there capable of thinking for himself."

"When I think of the Ymirans I've met," Ram said quietly, "I begin to wonder if Bassett might not be doing them a favor if he went ahead unchecked."

"They are a bunch of frigid, unthinking dullards, aren't they?" Counce agreed. "But look at it this way. No amount of external examination will reveal the solution to the Ymiran problem. No one except ourselves could realize its true nature. Bassett would doubtless think that to get his hands on a native Ymiran, study him, drain his mind of every subjective impression he recalls, would enable him to solve the problem. When he finds that's not enough after all, the letdown may be sufficient for him to give in and call on us for help."

"It strikes me as being very feasible," said Ram. "But for one thing. How do you propose getting such an Ymiran to Bassett?"

"Ask Jaroslav. If anyone can manage it, he can. He's told us that not all the younger generation on Ymir are as mentally fogbound as their elders. We must bring one of the most alert young people to Earth — by orthodox ship. If Bassett found memories of travel by transfax in the subject's mind, he'd recognize our hand in the matter and know he was being fooled."

"This isn't going to be exactly a pleasant experience for the Ymiran Jaroslav selects, is it?" put in Falconetta.

"Very unpleasant. But Jaroslav is about due to become the first, as distinct from the *only,* recruit we've had from Ymir. If he hasn't a suitable person in mind, I'll have some very unkind comments to make. But if he has, then I think the person he sends will be more than compensated for what he has to undergo by joining us later."

"Fair enough," nodded Falconetta. Counce glanced at Ram, and after a moment the white head inclined in agreement.

"Right. I'll go arrange it with Jaroslav," said Counce, pulling himself to his feet. "Ram, can you get enough power on this transfax to ship me to Ymir?"

"It's not the transfax that's the problem, but the propulsor pile of the submersible," said Ram dubiously. "This will probably drain its fissiles past their half-life. But I suspect the urgency justifies it. Please go ahead."

He rose from his chair and gave his habitual courtly bow; Falconetta smiled and lifted one slim beringed hand in salutation. In the middle of his own parting gesture, Counce found himself under a different sun.

CHAPTER V

TEMPERAMENTALLY, reflected Bassett, Lecoq and himself were ill-suited. If only he could find another man with such a gift for improvisation, but without Lecoq's irascibility and tendency to work himself up into a frenzy . . . He dismissed the thought. He had looked hard and long for a substitute for Lecoq, but, though Bassett was always careful not to let him know it, Lecoq had made himself indispensable.

Now he raised a hand to cut short the subordinate's flow of words. "Lecoq!" he said sharply. "Sit down, have a cigar, and shut up for a moment. Suppose we look at this matter with a bit more detachment—"

"Detachment!" snarled Lecoq. "With a situation like this facing us, how can we even pretend to be detached?"

"I said shut up and sit down," Bassett repeated levelly, and Lecoq, grumbling, subsided.

For a moment Bassett did not go on. He turned his head to the picture window at the right of his desk; made of one-way glass for privacy, it gave him a view from the vantage point of the eleventh floor clear across Rio to the edge of the sea. Afternoon sun was glimmering on a seeming infinity of windows in the lower buildings within his view.

Matter transmitter . . . The concept ticked through Bassett's mind. With instantaneous transport of goods, how enormously complex a trading empire might be built up; how much more of the visible universe might be delivered into the hands of man!

He grew aware that he was stretching Lecoq's limited ability to remain silent beyond its capacity. He turned back to face his assistant across the vast bare top of his enormous desk.

"You panic, Lecoq," he said bluntly. "As you say, it is disturbing to discover that there exists a group of persons with such resources that they can not only employ devices we believed to be purely hypothetical, but can also forecast the failure of a plan we believed to be reliable."

"Disturbing!" Lecoq snapped. "It means that we've been made monkeys of!"

"Nonsense. If this group, whoever they are and wherever they may operate from, were powerful enough for us to need to fear them, actively fear then, then they would not feel a need to remain hidden from us. Obviously, they do wish to stay concealed. This argues that they have considerable resources of knowledge, but not of effective forces. Yet it is reassuring that they have not succeeded in remaining in hiding. Up till the other day, we had heard the vaguest rumours of such a group. Now we know a good deal about them. Logically, I deduce that we have worried them out of their preferred pattern of behavior. Good. Let's do it again. Soon."

Lecoq scowled gloomily. "How? We still don't know where they operate, who their members are. I've consulted a dozen of our staff physicists, and none of them can define a method of detecting the operation of a matter transmitter, so we can't locate them that way."

"How?" said Bassett, ignoring the last part of Lecoq's

remark. "Why, by taking them at their word and capitalizing on their suggestion about Ymir."

"You're not seriously proposing to follow that up, are you?" Lecoq demanded. "Ymir! It's the least likely of the outworlds to afford a solution to our problems."

"They were right about our failure on Boreas, weren't they?" Bassett countered. "You're not going to tell me they rigged our own company computers to give us a false answer. No, we got adequate confirmation on that score as soon as we processed our data. Boreas is out. It looked obvious. This suggests to me that we probably weren't even asking the right questions. But that's beside the point. If this mysterious group has such exact knowledge of my personal movements, for example, that they can have a man waiting for me in mid-Pacific within half a mile of the place where my ship comes down—"

"They probably extrapolated from its entry into the atmosphere and transmitted the man there a moment before we arrived." Lecoq plainly did not think highly of the achievement.

"I don't care how he got there." Bassett hunched himself forward in his chair and rested his elbows on the desk. "The important fact is that they did have someone waiting to meet me on my arrival on Earth, which argues a close study and pretty full knowledge of my recent activities. No one except ourselves knew just when we were returning to Earth, nor that I was proposing to put down in mid-Pacific instead of coming direct to the South Atlantic off Rio, as might have been expected. That's point one.

"Point two: they knew in advance, and our computers have agreed with them, that Boreas was a stupid place to look for an answer to our problems.

"Point three: Despite their vaunted pretensions to be

able to solve the Ymiran problem, they took the trouble of arranging an elaborate and impressive means of telling me about it. This could well imply that they are in fact looking to me for the solution which they can't find, even though they know where it lies. Consequently—"

Bassett threw himself back in his chair again and gave Lecoq a belligerent and authoritative stare. "Consequently, we will investigate, with all the resources at our disposal. And this time we'll frame our questions differently. What do you know about Ymir, Lecoq?"

The suddenness with which he threw out the question took Lecoq by surprise. Now he hunted for his voice as if, in the unaccustomedly long period of listening, he had momentarily mislaid it.

"Why, I know quite a lot about all the colonies. Ymir is by far the coldest, most miserable and generally unlikely world which men have ever attempted to make their home. The equatorial regions are habitable; the population is around eight or ten million, and everyone is half-frozen and half-starved. But they claim to like it."

"No!" exploded Bassett. "That's a dangerous way of putting it. They don't *like* it; they endure it more or less gladly, and there's a whole universe of difference. I've been reading up on Ymir's history—just before I called you up, as a matter of fact. I still have the spool in, in fact."

He glanced down at the controls on the side of his desk, moved one of the switches, and shaded the windows so that the office was in half-darkness. Lecoq swung his chair around to face the same wall as Bassett, and on which, as the projector warmed up to speed, a flickering series of words and pictures appeared. Bassett was running the spool back to its beginning.

"This is an official account from the Ymiran Embassy,"

he said. "I had someone call on them and pick it up this morning. Apparently they supply these to anyone who asks for one, by way of publicity."

'I shouldn't have thought they had much to boast about on their icebox of a planet," Lecoq said sarcastically.

"Oh, it isn't boasting. It's probably a sort of inverted pride; they're displaying their toughness, self-righteousness and endurance. Look at that, now." He stopped the projector on a wide-angle shot of Ymir's capital city, Festerburg; its square, ugly buildings poked up between walls of ice, and coarse black smoke swirled about each rooftop, as if trying to blend it back into the bleak landscape. They burned coal and oil, laid down in an earlier interglacial period, obtained by arduous hand mining and drilling.

"Know where that is?" Bassett demanded.

"That's the capital," Lecoq snapped. "Festerburg."

"Right. Know why they call it Festerburg? It's from the first line of one of their religious songs, *Ein' feste Burg ist unser Gott*. I could think of better reasons for choosing the name, but that's the official reason as given here."

He snapped rapidly through a series of shots of the founding fathers of Ymir, all without exception angry-faced, intolerant-looking men and women. He stopped at a faded view of the original landing.

Among the glaciers and the snowdrifts, the peaked-faced children stood shivering while their parents held a ceremony around the ruins of the ships which had brought them. They were determined to cut every link that bound them to sinful, worldly, unspiritual Earth.

"Only they couldn't, of course," said Bassett. "They now refer to the fact under the excuse of wishing to go back and persuade us lush-living Earthers that we should deny the flesh as the Ymirans do. In fact, of course, they bit off more than they could chew. They intended to be self-sufficient and go ahead and mortify themselves in isolation; they managed to starve a few thousand children to death, and then they reopened limited contact with Earth, for seeds, ultrahardy meat animals, and so on. Well, that's been the way things have remained. The Ymirans maintain that it is hateful to them to spend a tour here at their embassy around the corner; they say they are nauseated by the luxury and fleshpots of Rio. In actual fact, I gather they line up for the jobs that fall vacant, and a few years ago one of their staff, a man called Jaroslav Dubin, actually fell, and started to mix with Earthmen as if we were perfectly acceptable. They had to ship him home quickly before he infected any of his colleagues. You won't find that mentioned in the official brochures, by the way.

"Their pose of denying themselves even the comfort of a tolerable climate because comfort of any kind is sinful is, as you may expect, beginning to slip. The elders, who are too set in their ways ever to change, would dearly like to cut all ties with Earth again and return to the original aims of the colonizers. Only they can't—not that we'd worry much if they did, mark you.

"However, as long as there is contact between the two planets, the younger generation on Ymir wonders, in spite of all, whether their revered ancestors *were* such righteous vessels of divine inspiration, or whether they were just a bunch of masochistic old fanatics bent on wrecking their descendants' future. Consequently, they detest us — for our sinfulness, they say, but more likely because they are profoundly, horribly, unsupportably jealous.

"To suggest to them that they should receive new immigrants from Earth is just as ridiculous as to think we'd ever find an Earthborn wanting to go there. This brings me back to my earlier point: we aren't asking the right questions."

"If this character with the matter transmitter isn't just feeding you a line because you were too close to a real solution on Boreas and he wanted to draw you off," said Lecoq brilliantly.

Bassett nodded. "I thought of that. That's why we're going to take Ymir and turn it upside down and shake it until the key factor falls out. If it's there. Right, Lecoq—you know what I want done. Get out and start doing it."

CHAPTER VI

ENNI ZATOK lived in a city. Everyone on Ymir lived in a city of which there were five on the entire planet. The reason was simple: comunal heating made the most of their exiguous resources of coal and oil, and in any case the mere presence of a concentrated mass of human bodies raised the temperature another valuable degree.

There were about ten million people on Ymir. The total had taken three centuries to reach that figure, for many children died young, and many adults, owing to poor nutrition and the adverse effects of the climate, were able to father only small families.

But Enni Zatok had seen pictures of people who went about in the open air with nothing on at all, under a sky as blue as her own eyes and a sun much more golden than her hair. She had compared their freedom of movement with her own, which was encumbered by layer on layer of protective clothing. She had drawn a conclusion. These people in the pictures bathed in a sea which glittered and glistened, and was so unlike the livid yellow-gray equatorial ocean hammering at the rocks of Ymir that Enni could not really convince herself that both were liquid water. She had drawn a conclusion from that too.

She had seen the pictures in a magazine from Earth, which belonged to Jaroslav Dubin. In fact, she had seen many books and magazines from Earth, and they all belonged to Jaroslav. But it was the pictures in the very first one which lived most vividly in her memory.

Jaroslav Dubin was not exactly famous on Ymir—rather, he was notorious, in a way that no one else had ever been. Because adults and prissy children always changed the subject when his name came up, his notoriety had grown and increased. Sometimes parents unwisely told their children of his awful fate as a cautionary tale—the story of the man who had sold his chance of salvation for the fleshpots of Earth — and consequently there were always boys and girls to snigger over what they knew about him.

One day a boy in her class at school confided that he had actually met the outcast Jaroslav, and that this miserable sinner was really the happiest, friendliest, most likeable person on the planet. When Enni timidly referred to the wiles of the devil, the boy went further in his admissions and furtively revealed that Jaroslav had given him a magazine which had actually been printed on Earth. The magazine revealed people living in the sinful luxury they had all heard described but had never seen.

Jaroslav, declared the boy who had met him, actually looked as happy as the people in the pictures — and to children accustomed to their sour-faced parents and teachers, that in itself was a minor miracle.

Enni looked longingly at the pictures. How could such people be the vessels of evil? Evil, she felt instinctively, must be dark and cruel and filthy, whereas these people were bright and gay and clean, and spoke kindly to one another.

She asked the boy who had the magazine to lend it to

her, and because not even the iron discipline of Ymiran society had been able to destroy certain fundamental reactions, and because Enni had an appealing smile and blue eyes and fair hair and was nearly seventeen years old, the boy had given her the magazine.

But she had made the mistake of hurrying to her room when she went home, to pore over the pages in private, and her father had come to see what she was up to. First he had tongue-lashed her; then he had torn precious pages to shreds and stamped on them; lastly he had made her take off her clothes and had left her for a night and a day and a night, naked, blue with cold, and without food or water, to impress the wickedness of her action on her.

Many things had been frozen into Enni's mind by those cold and lonely hours. Not least, her expression froze—into quiet obedience. Several times she heard her mother's footsteps approach, and hesitate outside the door as though she were going to ask how her daughter was. But every time she went away again without speaking. That too reinforced Enni's decision.

After it was all over, her father never mentioned what had happened. Certainly he would not have spoken about it to anyone outside the family; that would have been an admission of failure in his duty as a parent. A properly brought-up child should not even have felt the urge to commit such a sinful deed. Enni was glad of this, for she had to maintain an outward respect for her parents or be further punished. But behind her pale face her mind was very active.

For some time afterwards she was a model of good behavior. When a year had gone by without another breach of propriety, her parents again began to take her word for what she did, and that was the chance Enni had been waiting for — the chance to lie, to deceive, to cheat her parents on the grandest possible scale. How could she offer lip service to people she no longer regarded as fit to live?

In the meantime, in school and among her friends, there had been talk of Earth and the people of Earth, and also of Jaroslav Dubin, whose name was spoken in the hushed tones children of other worlds reserved for obscenities. Some of the children dared to voice the opinion that Jaroslav was right about the people of Earth and their parents were wrong; after all, they argued, Jaroslav had been to Earth and most people hadn't.

On the other hand, said the opposition, Jaroslav was the only one of many Ymirans who had been to Earth or to local planets who asserted an opinion contrary to the accepted one. Enni listened silently to this discussion; she already knew what she thought. She felt her skin itch, pent as it was inside two vests, two pairs of bloomers, sweater, heavy socks, clumsy, enormous shoes, parka, scarf, headwear, till; she could barely walk for the weight of the load. And she bided her time.

One night, when she had begged a friend to give her an alibi, she went to see Jaroslav Dubin. It was hardly a surprise to her to find four of her classmates already in Jaroslav's home.

Dearly as the elders of Ymir would have liked to see him ostracized, or better still dead and buried, they could not rid themselves of Jaroslav Dubin. Unrepentant, impervious to the coals of fire they figuratively heaped on his head, Jaroslav had taken advantage of the voyage home from Earth to get acquainted with the commander of the vessel on which he was shipped out. Afterwards, the elders wished they had not been so concerned to get Jaroslav off Earth before it was noised around that an Ymiran had actually deserted his fellows and gone off to live among the sinners of Earth. If they had not been in such a panic, they might have averted the consequences. On arriving on Ymir, the skipper of the spaceship informed the elders that Jaroslav Dubin was the only halfway human person he had met from what he called—as did most outsiders—this icebox of a planet. In the future he wanted Jaroslav to be his agent on Ymir; he was getting sick of having to face the frozen-gutted elders, and he wanted someone passably pleasant to deal with.

The elders refused; they could not conceive of doing otherwise. But the next ship that called refused to discharge cargo unless Jaroslav acted as agent.

The elders turned down the request, and set their jaws grimly. But the captain of the ship kept his word and took his cargo back into space as he had threatened. They missed three cargoes in identical circumstances. Plainly, there was a conspiracy; equally plainly, the Ymirans would have to give in.

So now, hated but tolerated, Jaroslav Dubin was plump and well-fed with supplies his friends of the space trade brought specially for him. It was these same spacemen, doubtless, who kept him provided with the ceaseless flow of additions to his library that he was so generous in lending out. Aching, cursing, the elders realized that in their midst they had a one-man subversive organization, about which they could do nothing.

They had even debated killing Jaroslav for the good of the community at large as they saw it. But the hard facts remained: the spacemen could get by without Ymiran trade, while Ymir could not survive without the spacemen's services. And if they could not satisfy the sharp minds of spacemen about the reason for Jaroslav's disappearance, they had no doubt the spacemen would withdraw their trade.

This, then, was the man Enni stole away to visit—not the sniveling outcast aware of his impending damnation that the elders would have liked to believe him, but the happiest, most comfortable individual on Ymir.

Enni had been working herself up to the visit for a year; her excited anticipation diluted her terror as she stole through the bare, icy streets, between the black, blank-faced houses, fearing at any moment to hear the tread of a custodian who would demand what she was doing out of her parents' home, and to whom lying would be of no use. It was worst of all when she came to the spaceport, for the elders had decreed that Jaroslav's house must be isolated from the city proper by a half mile of bare ground. But it was winter-dark, and no one saw her as she fled across the open space and cowered into the shelter of Jaroslav's porch.

It was warm, for Jaroslav had heating units that his friends in the space trade had given him; there was luscious off-world food and brilliant light. And there was talk — terrifying, wonderful talk, of Ymir and Earth, of Astraea and Boreas and K'ung-fu-tse and all the other worlds where men lived in greater comfort and happier surroundings than here.

Plump, smiling, as friendly as the descriptions Enni had been given, Jaroslav leaned back in a soft armchair, presiding over the discussions without saying much himself; his function was rather to generate ideas and leave them to be turned over in the minds of his companions. On that first evening Enni said nothing; she was self-conscious and embarrassed, because it was far too hot in Jaroslav's room to keep on her usual indoor clothes and no one but her parents had ever before seen her in her vest and bloomers. Later, she went again and talked a little, and then again, and then at every opportunity.

Sometimes she was the only person there aside from Jaroslav; sometimes there was a spaceship officer calling on his only friend on Ymir. Most often, though, the group consisted of three or four other young people who had managed to elude parental supervision for a precious hour or two.

On her third visit, Jaroslav, beaming delightedly, gave her a dress from Earth to put on while she was in the house, and thereafter he kept it waiting for her to change into on her arrival. She would never have dared to try and hide it in her own home.

After a while she found herself hoping that Jaroslav would be alone when she called. Occasionally he was. But he invariably treated her with courtesy and never presumed on the situation. She could not quite decide whether he wanted to or not at first. Later she learned to notice the slight disappointment in his manner as the evening progressed, if no one else turned up, and she realized that to Jaroslav an evening when he had only one visitor was a failure. Like leaven working in rising dough, Jaroslav's nature was to be yeast in the ferment of ideas now bubbling through the minds of the young men and women of Ymir.

And what did he get out of it? What was his purpose in this genuinely dangerous activity? Those were questions Enni found herself unable to answer. The danger lay in the possibility of the elders, or someone else in authority, discovering what was happening; then, whether or not Jaroslav himself suffered, his "pupils" would certainly be severely punished, and Enni had come wonderingly to understand that such an event would cause Jaroslav deep and sincere sorrow.

That, perhaps more than anything else about Jaroslav, reinforced the conclusions Enni had come to earlier. In her opinion, the fact that Jaroslav had learned (presumably among the people of Earth, for he had had no other chance) to care as deeply for the fate of others as for himself was the most astonishing thing about his altogether surprising nature. She told him so, one evening when no one else was with them, and for a long time the speculative look that came and went in his eyes as he listened haunted her memory and filled her mind with puzzlement.

Much later, she came to understand.

CHAPTER VII

THERE WAS more to Jaroslav Dubin's house than its mere
appearance. The elders, grudgingly, had assigned it to him
because they felt he would be less dangerous if he were
isolated from the rest of the population, quarantined by the
gap separating his one-story house of black stone from
the edge of the spaceport and the town itself. That had
suited Jaroslav fairly well. Every time the elders came to
see their self-appointed trading agent, the envy in their
eyes grew, for there was always something new to add to
the luxury Jaroslav enjoyed; a picture, a carpet, a piece of
furniture, rare offworld delicacies. They had objected
feebly to the crates of goods the spacemen brought for
their friend on Ymir, but they could not do more.

Envy was reflected, too, in the eyes of the young people
who called unofficially at the house — the youths and girls
like Enni Zatok. But that was as it ought to be. That was
why Jaroslav went to such pains to make his luxury osten-
tatious.

It was seldom, therefore, that he had a visitor who
merely accepted his surroundings. When such a visitor
came, he never came by the orthodox route; he always
came through the wall. The wall was cunningly hollowed

out; into the cavity led the power cables from the portable atomic generator he had installed below the main room. You needed a lot of power for operating a transfax platform.

He sat alone reading when the alarm sounded. The soft buzzing could have heralded anything — the arrival of a scrap of paper with a message on it, the delivery of a new batch of books and magazines, food, clothes. The things he used did not all by any means come by the regular space routes.

But when he opened the concealed wall panel and looked into the ten-foot cavity, he was startled to see a man.

"Saïd Counce!" he exclaimed, taking half a step back. "What in the galaxy brings you here? Come out and sit down."

Counce nodded and walked forward. He was still dressed as he had been for his visit to Bassett, in nothing but a pair of shorts, but Jaroslav kept his home warm and the pile carpets were kind to bare feet.

Hospitably bustling to fetch his guest a glass of wine and something to eat, Jaroslav hurried about the room while Counce chose a chair and looked musingly about him. There was a depth-illusion mobile on the whole of one wall, showing the local galaxy and the human-occupied worlds. There was a cosmopolitan selection of *objets d'art*. There were books and magazines that by Ymiran standards were intolerably seditious. That was all right.

He took the wine, refused any food, and indicated with a nod of his head that Jaroslav should take a chair facing him. When the plump man had done so, he looked him straight in the eye.

"Jaroslav, what have you been doing lately?" he demanded.

"Spreading the word. I've been working under the most

47

extreme difficulties, as usual. But the work is paying off. I wish there were several agents here on Ymir instead of myself alone."

"So do we all," Counce agreed. "Only until we think of an excuse as brilliant as the one which forced the elders to tolerate you, we can't establish more people here. It's a peculiar trait of human psychology that one misfit will be tolerated as a crank when two or more automatically assume the status of a subversive movement. Originally, the plan was for you to act as a focus of infection. You don't seem to have made yourself very contagious."

Jaroslav blinked. "I think I've done tolerably well under the circumstances," he objected. "In the five years I've been here, I've managed to get thousands of books and magazines into surreptitious circulation. I have regular visitors among the young people — some of them are even bold enough to smile at me on the street now."

"We're facing a desperate situation. We have to take risks. Why, for instance, have you not recommended anyone as a recruit yet?"

"Mainly because the only people I've made any serious impression on have been boys and girls in their early teens. Ymiran conditioning is hellishly successful; by the time the children reach adult status at eighteen, they're solid from the neck up."

"I've never worked on Ymir," said Counce thoughtfully. "But I have worked on more than twenty different worlds. I think you're still partly a victim of your own early conditioning yourself, despite what we did to counteract it. There are ten million people on the planet. In five years it ought to be possible to find more than one person with sufficient hereditary empathy to free him or her from his background. You were a white-haired boy at one time, remember? When the elders selected you to join the staff of their embassy on Earth, you were regarded as totally uncorruptible. You fell inside the year. Agreed, you were exposed to the truth at first hand. But though you're working with diluted information, you've had a much longer time and many more people to work on. I want a potential recruit, Jaroslav — and I want him *now*."

Jaroslav's eyes searched his visitor's face. "You have bad news, Saïd," he suggested.

"I have." Counce put his glass down and got to his feet. "The Others have been to Regis. They were there before we arrived — possibly only scouting the planet, possibly with the intention of planting a colony. We don't know for sure. But we've got to hurry."

He put his thumb on a certain star in the pattern on the wall-map. 'That's Regis, Jaroslav. And here" — he made a pair of compasses with his forefinger and thumb, and swung the finger through a third of a circle — "is Ymir. Ymir is the sort of world the Others hunt for. Oxygen-high, frigid, almost lifeless, it's virtually perfect for them. The worst danger we can conceive of is that they should chance across it.

"We thought they had been concentrating their efforts in a direction at right angles to Ymir. But if they've come as close as Regis once, they may come again. They may come at any time."

He turned round and faced Jaroslav again. "Well?" he said.

"Working here on Ymir is like trying to plod through knee-deep mud. A dozen times I've had my eye on potential recruits, only to find — almost from one week to the next — that their defense against the received pattern of thinking here on Ymir is faulty, and they've succumbed. From being a trusted friend I turn overnight into an emissary of the devil. You say you want a potential recruit now.

The only one I can honestly recommend is a girl, aged seventeen or so. And she probably isn't mature enough to be of use."

"She'll have to do," said Counce grimly. "Who is she?"

"Her name is Enni Zatok. Her father is in the power station; he's a charge hand or overseer, I believe. He's an infernal bigot, and probably in another ten years he'll qualify for an elder's post through sheer blockheadedness. But the girl came to me of her own accord, and she's kept on coming for a year. I think she has real possibilities."

"She'll do as a start. I want you to get her to Earth as fast as you can — by orthodox shipping routes. That's essential. When she gets there, I'm going to arrange that Bassett should hear about her, get hold of her, and pick her mind clean of information about Ymir." He gave a brief summary of the events that had led up to his decision.

Jaroslav whistled. "It sounds like a thin chance. How thin?"

Counce spread his hands and shook his head. "It's the best we've got, and it'll have to be tried. Can you do it?"

"Give me a moment to think it out," Jaroslav requested, and sat back in his chair and closed his eyes.

Counce waited impatiently. After a minute, Jaroslav got hastily to his feet and crossed the room to consult a pile of papers. He riffled through them, and then, holding his fingers in the pile to mark the place, said over his shoulder, "Will eight days from now be soon enough?"

"To get this girl off Ymir? No, not nearly."

"To get her to Earth is what I mean. She could leave on the *Amsterdam* — Captain Leeuwenhoek was the man who brought me back from Earth, my first and best friend among the spacecrews. He isn't scheduled to touch Earth this trip, but it wouldn't lose him anything to scrap his schedule for once."

"Good," said Counce succinctly. "Anything else?"

"Lord, yes! For one thing, although I've managed to convince Enni pretty thoroughly of the fact that Earthborn people aren't invariably cruel and wicked, I doubt if she would voluntarily sever her ties with Ymir. After all, she still suffers the standard Ymiran family conditioning; deep down in her mind her father, bloody though he may be, is still a sort of god-figure. I'll have to think up a pretty strong threat to make her give in."

"Any ideas?"

"She's been here on her own several times — I could make out that the elders have discovered the fact and will beat her into confessing that I seduced her. They would, too, if they had the chance. I saw one of the local misfits being whipped naked through the streets the other day. He'd missed three consecutive confession-meetings. I had to run out of sight, or I'd have tried to grab the whip or something. This is a hell of a place, Saïd."

"Of course it is! This planet simply isn't fit for human beings to live on. That's the fundamental postulate behind all our present plans." He mused for a moment. "Could you get her aboard the *Amsterdam* and off-world before anyone discovered she was missing?"

"Certainly. Enni herself could arrange that. She manages to alibi herself for two or three hours at a time twice a week or so, anyway, and by the time her parents got tired of sitting grimly by the door waiting to whip her for staying out late, she could be clear of the planet. You've no idea how much they'd love to whip her. The hope of doing so will keep them from worrying where she's gone for at least an extra three or four hours."

Counce gave Jaroslav a long, steady look. "Jaroslav, you seem to be letting this place get you down. You'd better clear your mind a little. After all, no matter how repulsive the Ymirans' behavior is, you're an Ymiran yourself. You're a human being and so are they. Once you stop recognizing that fact, consciously and continuously, you're a failure. We've had failures occasionally. We had to stop them. I'm not threatening you — just reminding you."

Jaroslav gave a weary smile. "Don't worry, Saïd. That's my own kith and kin I'm insulting; I think I have a better right to know what's wrong with them than an off-worlder, no matter how highly developed his empathy. What we need here, Saïd, is some method of exposing the youngsters firsthand to a different environment. Enni will be lucky; you'll take her on if she survives the experience with Basset —"

"We will. We couldn't forgive ourselves if we didn't."

Jaroslav nodded. "In the end, anyway, she'll get her facts straight. She'll be a decent, functioning human being. But she'll only be one."

"Organize it, then! Damn it, that's what you're here for. Arrange wholesale stowing away aboard the spacecraft that call here. Kidnap a whole street gang or something — you can cover yourself. Pinch a hundred boys and girls from their beds with your transfax, drug them, and let them wake up on Shiva or Zeus or K'ung-fu-tse. Wouldn't the spacemen play?"

"Not very likely. We need agents working in the spacecrews too, you know."

"Spacecrews are the least of our worries. They see all the different worlds, and can enjoy themselves equally anywhere. They're tolerant. They're spacemen first and men second, and that's close enough to what we want. We couldn't waste the effort."

"But couldn't we recruit people like Leeuwenhoek, for instance?"

"We could. Try it yourself when he's here; if he seems likely, ask him to quit his ship and send him to Regis. I'll tell Wu to expect him."

Counce swigged the last of his wine. "Well, good-bye, Jaroslav. I'm sorry I can't stay longer. But I'll have to make sure that a certain Ymiran teen-age girl, who arrives on Earth in eight days' time, falls into the right hands — and that's going to mean having every third person on the docks on our side during the crucial hour or two. You think you have problems? Try mine sometime!"

They exchanged understanding and mutually forgiving grins, and then Counce was gone.

CHAPTER VIII

HER PARENTS might not have noticed the piece of paper in the bare, chilly room. They seldom came in here. Enni was charged with cleaning it and making her own bed, and she, like most other young people on Ymir, had very few personal belongings. Occasionally, she knew, her father looked in late at night to see that she was properly in bed and asleep.

But she knew every inch of the floor, the walls and the ceiling, so that when she came in and set her schoolbooks down, the out-of-place whiteness was the first thing that caught her eye.

She picked it up. She had seen enough of Jaroslav Dubin's handwriting to recognize that this sample was genuine. With harsh fear clutching at her throat, she read:

Enni, you and I are in terrible danger. Come and see me this evening. Jaroslav.

Terror, the fear of discovery and its certain consequences, had walked day and night with Enni for many months. She didn't stop to wonder how the note had got where it was, whether it might in fact be a forgery designed to provoke her into giving away a damaging fact. Thankful that she had not yet taken off her outdoor clothes, she turn-

54

ed and went straight back into the street.

She had not spoken to her mother, who was in the kitchen; her father would be working late tonight at the power station. With luck, she could get to Jaroslav's and back before her absence was noticed. *With luck*. She was too scared to think beyond that point.

Usually Jaroslav greeted her at the door of his home and showed her into the small anteroom where she could change into her treasured dress from Earth before joining him in the lounge. Tonight he brought her straight through to the main room. There was a stranger there.

Sweating in her heavy clothes, Enni stood shifting from foot to foot, aching to know what the danger was that Jaroslav had written about, while the strange man — tall and bearded — looked her over thoughtfully. The pause grew unbearable.

"Enni," said Jaroslav at last, "this is Captain Leeuwenhoek of the space trader *Amsterdam*. He's a very close friend of mine, and he may be able to save us from appalling danger."

Leeuwenhoek nodded and gave a mechanical smile.

"The situation's this," said Jaroslav. "The elders have found out that you've been coming here on your own. They're planning to arrest you at home tonight and beat you until you confess that I have seduced you."

On Ymir, no one used words as frank as "seduce"; Enni felt a vast blush heat her skin, making the already great warmth intolerable. She said, "But that wouldn't be true!"

Jaroslav just looked at her, and she rushed on, "But you can't mean that the *elders* would lie like that!"

The spaceman, sitting at Jaroslav's side, coughed and spoke for the first time. "With due respect, miss, your elders have a reputation for being the finest liars in the galaxy. Ask anyone who has to do business with them.

They're so self-righteous they end up by convincing themselves they're telling the truth."

"But it wouldn't be a lie, so far as they're concerned," Jaroslav said quietly. "People like that are only prepared to believe the worst of their fellow men, because they're only capable of the worst themselves. They suspect, and in their hearts they're sure, that I've done evil to you. They would beat you until you lied to save yourself more pain. Then they would have the chance they have so long sought to destroy me."

Leeuwenhoek chipped in, "You see, young woman, Jaroslav here is a friend of us spacemen. We'd make damned sure your elders did nothing to him groundlessly. But we couldn't say a word if he'd really—uh—taken advantage of you. According to Ymiran law they'd have a case against him, all right, and we would have to admit it. We're honest. Have to be. The elders know it."

Enni made vague waving gestures, and they interpreted the motion correctly and fell silent to let her think. After a pause, she said, tears trembling in her eyes, "But Jaroslav, what can we do?"

"There's only one thing to be done," said Jaroslav brutally. "Get you out of the elders' reach."

"How? There's nowhere I could go without people asking questions, and the news would get back —"

"Nowhere on Ymir," said Jaroslav. "But you've often said you wanted to see other worlds, Enni. Here's your chance. The *Amsterdam* is due to lift in two hours. You'll have to be aboard."

Enni's eyes grew suddenly round and wide with horror. "I couldn't," she whispered. "I just couldn't."

"You'll have to," said Jaroslav. "Either you go, or you wait until the elders send a custodian around to fetch you. They'll whip the skin off your back to start with. If you still don't tell them what they want to hear, they'll put salt on the cuts. After that, they'll hang you head first over a barrel of ice water and duck you until you're blue. You've seen heretics on trial — you know what would happen."

She knew. She had taken the fifteen-year-old's classes in citizenship. She had seen the solemn men and women in black attending to heretics and backsliders, while the children were urged to sing louder and drown the victims' cries. There was fear enough to drive a thousand to flight.

Urging her the same way were a host of memories of what she had learned from Jaroslav; her own longing to walk under a warm and grateful sun set in a clear blue sky, to move unencumbered by the Ymiran garments which now were like an oven on her body. If she had been alone with Jaroslav, she would have felt sufficiently unself-conscious to take some of them off; Ymiran conditioning, though, still hung so heavily on her that she could not think of removing even her outermost parka in the presence of a total stranger.

And Ymir was with her in other ways too. There was more than the fear; there were the threats and the promises. In the back of her mind a small voice was whispering that maybe a beating from the elders was compensation for her guilt in lying to her parents, in visiting the proscribed Jaroslav. Maybe this was her just due, which would have to be borne in silence and even joy so that she could be cleansed and receive a second chance.

The stern, righteous men leaped up behind her closed eyelids, to glare at her accusingly. They had sought her out and discovered her wickedness —

But Leeuwenhoek had said these just, upright persons were reputed the finest liars in the galaxy. She opened her eyes again and gave the spaceman a puzzled look. He seemed, he sounded like, a decent man. It was hard to believe that he would lie.

The indecision made Enni's mind whirl; the heat was overpowering. A spasm of giddiness blurred her vision. She put her hand to her face and then tried to seize a support to stop herself from falling.

She did not become completely unconscious until she had measured her length on the floor. It was for this reason that she was able to hear Jaroslav say in a satisfied tone, "Good. She's fainted."

But she had no time to be properly astonished at this remark before blackness swamped her mind.

"Are you all right now?"

It was a woman's voice, deep and anxious. Enni listened to it with puzzlement because it was not quite right. The words were oddly accented, but nonetheless in a familiar way.

Of course. Leeuwenhoek, and some of the other spacemen she had met at Jaroslav's, spoke with such an accent, distinct from the Ymiran one. She turned her head from contemplating the plain white ceiling, and saw a brown-haired woman at the side of the bed.

"Are you Mrs. Leeuwenhoek?" she asked.

"No, I'm the ship's doctor," the woman answered with a smile. She wore white coveralls and there were shiny metal instruments showing from her pockets. "You must be recovered now; that's the first question you've asked."

Enni pondered. She was in a bed softer than her own, and the air was so warm she had nothing over her except a single coverlet. She felt amazingly free and unrestrained. Inspection told her that this was due to having no clothes on.

The coverlet came all the way to her shoulders, and the

doctor was a woman; nonetheless, Enni felt herself going scarlet.

"Do you know where you are?" the doctor asked gently.

Enni nodded. She knew. Somewhere in the immediate past was the strangest, most confused memory of her young life. Black, menacing figures had started up at her from every corner; she had tried wildly to run from them, to strike at them and beat them down. Some of them had held whips. The heat had been feverish and intolerable, and she had not been able to eat or drink for fear the food or water might be poisoned. But out of the confusion certain things had become clear to her. That she was aboard a ship; that the ship was taking her away from the horrors lurking in wait on Ymir; and her thinking was as clear as spring water.

"What really happened?" she whispered.

"First of all you fainted in Jaroslav Dubin's house. When Captain Leeuwenhoek brought you aboard, you were still unconscious; then it turned out that you'd picked up a fever. You've been in a coma for four days and nights. But that's all over now."

The doctor slapped the edge of the bed reassuringly and got to her feet. "You'll feel a bit weak for the moment, but we'll feed you up and make you better than new."

She hesitated, looking down at the pale-faced girl in the bed. "Enni, how do you feel about — about what's happened to you?"

"About coming away from Ymir, do you mean?" Enni asked with composure. "I don't quite know. I feel I ought to be terribly scared, only I'm not."

"That's because we gave you some tranquilizer shots while you were ill. They'll wear off."

"Will I feel differently then?" Enni sounded genuinely puzzled.

"Yes, quite differently. But — maybe I shouldn't say this; still, I'm going to — you damned well ought to feel glad. I heard what you were screaming about while you were delirious. How old are you, Enni? fifteen?"

"Nearly eighteen," said Enni with slight indignation. The doctor ignored the indignation, and went on.

"Just as bad. What a *hell* of a place Ymir must be, if all poor kids like you get their heads stuffed with the sort of evil nonsense you were spewing up while you were feverish. The galaxy would be a cleaner place if people like that were disinfected out of existence. They're as bad as germs!"

"I don't understand," frowned Enni. Surely the doctor couldn't be talking about *Ymirans* with such loathing?

The doctor laughed, and patted Enni's fair hair. "You just relax, little one. I'll go get you something to set you up."

Little one. Enni had never thought of herself that way; indeed, she was regarded as tall for her age. But now that she considered the matter, she realized that the doctor would be taller than herself by at least fifteen inches. And the spacemen who called on Jaroslav — they were inches taller than he was, too.

It affected her more profoundly than anything had before, to learn from the doctor when she returned that the Ymirans, the self-appointed, self-righteous Ymirans, owing to malnutrition and the rigors of climate, were in actual fact the runts of the whole human race.

"Discovery of Ymir by the Others," the old man said.

Here's Max.

The maximum 120mm cigarette.

**Great tobaccos. Terrific taste.
And that long, lean,
all-white dynamite look.**

*"Max, I can take
you anywhere."*

© Lorillard 1976

After all I'd heard I decided to either quit or smoke True.

I smoke True.

King Regular: 11 mg. "tar", 0.6 mg. nicotine;
00's Menthol: 13 mg. "tar", 0.7 mg. nicotine
av. per cigarette FTC Report Nov. 1975.

The low tar, low nicotine cigarette.

Regular: 19 mg. "tar,"
1.3 mg. nicotine;
Menthol: 18 mg. "tar,"
1.3 mg. nicotine
av. per cigarette by
FTC Method.

Here's Max.

The maximum 120mm cigarette.

Great tobaccos. Terrific taste.
And that long, lean,
all-white dynamite look.

"Max, I can take you anywhere."

© Lorillard 1976

After all I'd heard I decided to either quit or smoke True.

I smoke True.

King Regular: 11 mg. "tar", 0.6 mg. nicotine;
100's Menthol: 13 mg. "tar", 0.7 mg. nicotine
av. per cigarette FTC Report Nov. 1975.

The low tar, low nicotine cigarette.

CHAPTER IX

THE SENSATION as the tranquilizer shots wore off was the most extraordinary Enni could remember. Like water leaking into a tank, apprehension began to flood gradually through her mind. They brought her food — strange to her, and hard for her to adjust to — and then offered her clothes to put on. In the matter of dress, Ymiran custom made modesty a necessity and nothing that she was shown really fulfilled the function of concealing the body, which subconsciously she still regarded as of prime importance. True, she had worn that dress from Earth in the privacy of Jaroslav's home — but that had had something of childish make-believe and "dressing up" about it; this was reality, a reality that grew more frightening as the minutes ticked away.

Shyly, she rejected the short-skirted frocks, the saris which Video India's influence had made so popular on Earth, the virtually translucent chitons from Zeus, and screwed up her courage enough to put on a suit of silky pajama-like garments from K'ung-fu-tse, which were the closest of all to the demanding standards of Ymiran modesty.

Timidly, feeling like a new arrival in a naturist colony,

knowing that she was not conspicuous and yet unable to rid herself of self-consciousness, she ventured to follow the doctor from the sick quarters.

"That's a good girl," the doctor approved. "I'll take you up to the bridge. Captain Leeuwenhoek has been asking after you."

"Where are we going?" Enni inquired after a moment trying desperately to keep up with the doctor's long strides.

"Going? Well, we aren't going anywhere any longer — we already went, as you might say. You've been out for four days, you know. We broached air just about the time you woke up."

The impact of what it meant to lose four days from one's life started to hammer at Enni's mind. They were going through a pipelike corridor, metal-walled; three or four members of the crew passed them, nodded to the doctor, gave Enni curious, searching glances.

"We weren't scheduled to come so far on this trip," the doctor was saying. "But we had to get you out of the reach of those elders of yours, and Jaroslav's a friend of ours — all of us in the space trade know him pretty well. That's a good man, you know! So we cut through straight to Earth."

Earth! The doctor was saying something explanatory about cargo costs and the reason why the extra long trip would not be a loss to the crew, but Enni could not hear for the thunder of blood in her ears.

It was one thing to dream about a pleasant world where people could live freely and enjoy their lives; quite another suddenly to find herself there. Earth, the wellspring of evil, the fountainhead of sin, the worst, most ill-famed planet in the galaxy — to an Ymiran, at least. The world from which the founding fathers had departed in scorn and hatred —

that was a tale every Ymiran schoolchild learned as soon as he or she could talk.

Blindly, she kept up with the doctor, not noticing the complex equipment lining the walls they now were passing, hardly noticing as they passed through a vacuum bulkhead into a place full of light and busy people.

"Hullo, Enni!" exclaimed Captain Leeuwenhoek from his post by the main control panels. Enni took no notice. A blinding, wonderful truth had burst in on her, and she was dazzled.

The bridge had been opened to the air. The screens had been rolled back, and through them came the gentle plopping sound of waves breaking against the hull of the ship. They had of course settled on water; it would have been suicide to attempt a landing on Ymir's gnaw-toothed, storm-racked oceans, but Earth's wide stretches of calm sea served better than land-built bases or the operating of spacecraft. Ahead was a city of splendid whiteness, set against a montage of green hills. Nearer, tugs were coming out to meet the *Amsterdam* and gentle her through the last few miles to the main docks.

Enni had never seen a city like Rio, nor such vessels as the powerful, shining-clean tugs. But she was not looking at either. She was looking at the sky, blue, warm, with a powdering of high white clouds, and at the sea, which rolled lazily in long undulations: gentle, green, inviting.

And to this, eyes bright, Enni was saying under her breath, "Why, it's true! It's really true!"

Behind her, Leeuwenhoek gave the doctor a significant glance; the doctor nodded and smiled.

Enni stayed on the bridge, not daring to miss a moment of what was going on, hardly speaking even when spoken to, until the tugs had urged the *Amsterdam* into dock, and the sight of the sea and sky had almost been obscured by the piled crates, the cranes and conveyors, the hulls of other docked vessels, and the sheersided warehouses fronting on the wharf. Everywhere there were people going about their business; everywhere there was noise and shouting.

And now Enni's delight gave way again to apprehension. It was so different, so vastly different from anything she had ever known. What would she do here on Earth? What *could* she do? How would people treat her? True, the men and women she could see on the dockside appeared friendly enough, and spoke in cheerful tones to each other; true, Jaroslav had told her that when he rebelled against the rules imposed on the staff of the Ymiran Embassy and went to meet Earthmen on their own ground, the reaction he got when he admitted his origin was something like, "Ymiran, huh? Thought you guys weren't allowed out on the streets, or something — we never see your people around. Have another drink."

But . . .

An official-looking person in a smart white uniform came to the dockside and shouted for the skipper; Leeuwenhoek went to lean out of the bridge port and discuss his cargo manifest and unloading arrangements. There was something about buyers coming around in an hour or two. Enni did not follow all that was said.

Leeuwenhoek finished his discussion and turned inboard with a tired but satisfied expression. "Well, we might as well step ashore for a few hours," he said. "Enni, you'd best come along and we'll fit you out with some things you need. Like the idea?"

Enni nodded.

Petr Tomlin had been a buyer for Bassett's for more than ten years. His beat included the Rio docks; sometimes off-world cargoes included miscellanea that could be resold at a ridiculously large profit after a suitable advertising campaign to drive home the glamorous aspect of their colonial origin.

When the *Amsterdam's* details went up on the main arrivals board, he scanned them with an expert eye. Ymir, last port of call. A god-forsaken, one-propulsor world, that. In all his experience, he'd never seen a decent cargo come off Ymir. Still, for some reason, during the past few days, interest had been growing in the firm; and, after all, the previous ports of call included two reliable worlds with occasional respectable exports.

Better drop by and take a look, he decided.

The cargo-master was a stranger to him, but he was expert at making friends quickly, and within the half-hour they were chatting amiably together. None of the competing buyers had yet made up their minds to inspect the *Amsterdam;* Tomlin allowed the cargo-master to expand a little before they settled down to serious business.

"We don't see you often in Rio," he suggested. "Does your beat usually include Earth?"

The cargo-master shook his head. "We work the outworlds most of the time. Nothing fancy — seeds, cattle stock in embryo, processed reactor fuels, that sort of thing. Only we had a special reason for calling on Earth this trip — last-minute change of plan, in fact."

Some instinct made Tomlin prick up his ears. "You don't say!" he prompted. The cargo-master decided to elucidate.

"Some girl from Ymir got herself in trouble with the local authorities. The agent there is a friend of the skipper's. He agreed to ship the girl out of the elders' reach as a favor to him."

"Pretty expensive sort of favor!" Tomlin commented.

"Not really. We figured it out before we started, and I think when you look at what we've got you'll see it would have been worth our while to make the trip anyway."

That was the signal for the start of serious business; all the time that Tomlin was haggling and making his offers, though, the question of why a single Ymiran girl should have been brought to Earth as a favor irked him. He mentioned it to his chief, Lecoq, when he reported in that night, and the reaction which the news provoked startled him.

"An Ymiran girl? Here in Rio? What's she like? How old is she? Where is she right now?"

Tomlin stammered feebly that he hadn't bothered to ask. Lecoq slammed his fist down on the desk and ordered him harshly to get out and find her. Then he countermanded the order and rang Bassett.

Bassett had been poring over yet another file of information on Ymir. It seemed to him that he was thinking of nothing else these days. And the more he studied the question, the more he suspected Lecoq had been right all along. Ymir was a ridiculous planet to try and reopen to immigration! It would take more than the impending crisis in living standards to drive Earthborn to Ymir; it would take a disaster.

Therefore, if they weren't completely off-beam, they were still asking the wrong questions.

It was a job for a social psychologist. He had recruited the best available to his staff, but they had nothing to work on. None of them had been to Ymir; there was no opportunity to meet and talk with members of the embassy staff in Rio, except on the most formal footing; Ymirans had no spacefleet and seldom visited other planets; and most certainly, they would refuse to co-operate if Bassett or anyone went direct to Ymir to study the problem at first hand.

Dead end.

They were making do with what they had — analysis of the semantic distortions in Ymiran official publications, for example, provided useful clues to their basic psychology. But what they really needed as Bassett was fully aware, was a complete understanding of the human situation on Ymir, as directly experienced by an individual citizen. Until they had that, they were fumbling in the dark.

Did Counce's boast about being able to handle the problem imply that his group had that kind of information? If the range of their matter transmitter was interstellar, that could be the case. Their agents could move among Ymirans while posing as natives; they would generate none of the hostility inspired by visiting spacemen.

That was why, when Lecoq rang him with the news of an Ymiran girl's arrival in Rio, he felt like getting up and doing a small dance of joy.

"Excellent!" he said crisply. "That's exactly the sort of opportunity we've been looking for. How soon can we track this girl down?"

"I'm intending to start at once," Lecoq answered. "I thought you'd want to know immediately."

"Right. But we'll have to handle this delicately. Here we've got a girl practically alone on a strange world, and if there's any truth in the survey reports I've read, she'll be scared to death of the sinfulness and wicked ways of Earthborn people. Uh — what was the name of that Ymiran who deserted the staff of the embassy a few years ago?"

"Jaroslav Dubin."

"Fine. We're friends of Jaroslav's, then, so far as she's concerned. Brief half a dozen sober, respectable-looking young female secretaries and make sure it's one of them who actually contacts her. Girls from these backward planets are usually scared blind of the opposite sex. Order them to gain her confidence gently, and then lure her here somehow. After that, we can let the psychologists take over. Better make sure nobody is supposed to meet her or look after her here."

"That's unlikely. It seems this was strictly a spur-of-the-moment arrangement. But I'll cover it, just in case."

"Good. Keep me in touch. And find the girl *fast*."

Bassett smiled in satisfaction as he leaned back in his chair. He would have been a good deal less pleased if he had known that Counce was also smiling, elsewhere in Rio, at precisely the same moment and over precisely the same events.

CHAPTER X

FOR AN ADULT, Enni decided there was something surprisingly childlike about Leeuwenhoek. His naïve delight in showing her about Rio was patent wherever they went. Enni fastened on it because it afforded her a sort of shield against the real problem facing her.

The *Amsterdam* would stay only a few days on Earth; time in port was costly in harbor dues and wasted voyage time. Somehow, between now and the ship's departure, she would have to make friends, get on her feet. There would be opportunity enough after that for sight-seeing. The fundamental trouble, of course, was that never in her young life had Enni done anything on her own, aside from stealing away to visit Jaroslav. She had never had hours to herself, to do with as she liked; idleness, the Ymirans declared, was also a sin.

Her heart sank steadily as the discovery of the complexity and unfamiliarity of life on Earth became more apparent with every step she took. Far from impressing and delighting her, Leeuwenhoek's parade of wonders depressed her, made her more and more uncertain of herself.

What had Jaroslav done to her, abandoning her like this on Earth?

Belatedly, Leeuwenhoek discovered that he should have been back at the docks half an hour ago; he rushed her to the ship and abandoned her temporarily on the wharf while he went to talk with a customs official.

Lonely, worried, trying to keep control of herself, Enni looked about her. Another ship was being pushed clear of an adjacent berth; beyond, the flaming trail of a ship blazing toward the sky struck across the ocean. It was so enormous, all of it, after the constriction and narrowness of Ymir, that her mind seemed unable to contain it.

A young woman, plain, soberly dressed in brown, walked as though in doubt toward the wharf. She looked for a few moments at the *Amsterdam;* catching sight of Enni, she turned and approached her.

"Excuse me. Do you know the name of this ship?" she asked.

"The — the *Amsterdam,*" said Enni, rather faintly. The young woman thanked her, but hesitated before turning away.

"You're a stranger, aren't you?" she suggested. "Have you just arrived?"

Enni nodded. "I'm from Ymir," she ventured, wondering what the reaction would be, but needing to prove for herself that Jaroslav had told her the truth.

"Why, how interesting!" The plain woman gave a friendly smile, and Enni felt a surging of relief. "You must have come in on the *Amsterdam,* then. I heard there was a ship from Ymir in Rio, so I came round to ask if anyone had news of a friend of mine. An Ymiran. I met him years ago, and I've never forgotten him. You might even know him, I guess — his name is Jaroslav Dubin."

"Of course I know him!" exclaimed Enni. "Why, what a

wonderful surprise to meet someone who actually is a friend of Jaroslav's!"

And she poured out the whole story of her panicky flight.

"Well!" said the plain woman when she had finished. "I never would have thought Jaroslav would do such a thing. I think it's awful, just sending you to Earth to save his own skin, and not doing anything to make sure you were all right. My name is Dolores Lourenço — call me Dolly. Where's this captain of yours? I think he deserves a talking-to for letting this happen!"

After that, things happened very rapidly. Enni's head whirled. Somehow, though, she found herself being whisked into a cab with her new-found friend, who announced that she was going to organize Enni's immediate future for her. Enni asked no questions about what was going on, for fear of appearing either stupid or ungrateful, and though she was puzzled to find herself being taken into a vast building in the center of the city, which certainly did not look like a place where people lived, she kept her thoughts to herself.

Men and women glanced at her — glanced *down* at her, she realized — and she tried not to be conscious of their eyes. Her clothing was unusual, but not extraordinary, so that could hardly be the reason for their interest. Her youth? Her smallness? She could not guess.

Her own eyes were otherwise occupied. The building they entered was gigantic beyond her dreams. Twenty or more floors reared up to the sky, paneled with glass and metal and plastics; strange carvings decorated the walls, sounds and smells that puzzled her filled the air. There was humming of machinery, barely noticeable.

So spacious! So wastefully spacious! On Ymir men cramped themselves and huddled together, yet there were only ten million people in the whole world. Here there were ten million in a single city, and everyone had room.

She was in a small compartment rather than a room, with Dolores; the compartment startled her by pressing its floor against her feet. An elevator; on Ymir, there were ladders and occasionally, if there was room, a flight of stairs.

A light corridor with numbered doors. Dolores took her through one of the doors, and a man at a table looked up. He had sharp, bright eyes under vast bushy eyebrows; he wore white coveralls like the doctor aboard the *Amsterdam*.

"I found her, Dr. Gold," Dolores said. "Right near the ship she came on. She's all yours."

Gold nodded, thrusting back his chair to get to his feet. "Thank you, Miss Lourenço. Sit down, please, young woman."

Startled, Enni glanced from the doctor to Dolores. "What — what's going on?" she faltered.

Dolores shrugged. "I only do as I'm told," she said. "I wouldn't know." Her face had lost its sympathetic expression, and now seemed quite hard and masklike. Enni felt an empty sensation of betrayal. She could not find her voice.

For a moment, Dolores' face softened again. "Good luck, kid, anyway. Don't be hard on her, will you, Doc?" she added over her shoulder, and then she was gone from the room.

"Sit down, please," Gold repeated. Enni took a deep breath.

"No. Not until you tell me what's going on!"

"You will do as you're told," said Gold bluntly. "You must understand that you are not very important."

Enni, biting her lip, shook her head in dismay rather

than refusal. "Very well," said Gold heavily, and pressed a knob on his desk. A door opposite the one by which Enni had entered slid aside, and more men, also in white coveralls, came in quietly. They moved toward Enni.

She screamed.

It was not long before she discovered that the tales the elders told about Earth were a mere fraction of the truth. With hypnotics and suggestion-drugs, they opened her mind, took possession of it, drained it of her most secret memories. They recorded her words and her screams and played them back until there was no corner of her brain to which she could flee for even an instant's privacy.

It seemed to go on for a long time. It seemed to go on forever.

Falconetta's house was built on the edge of the Indian Ocean — literally. At high tide, the sea flowed over the transparent ceiling of the main room. It was high tide now, and Falconetta and Ram Singh waited tensely in greenish luminescence. They hardly spoke. Every now and again they betrayed their impatience by gestures.

When at length the transfax alarm sounded, they started in spite of themselves. Falconetta leaped to her feet and went to open the concealed door of the cabinet. They always hid their transfax units; they had to. Strangers might otherwise have asked questions.

Counce came out into the room and answered their unspoken questions with a nod.

"He's got her. And they've probably already gone to work. Now we've got to figure out how long we can leave her in his hands."

"As short a time as possible," said Falconetta firmly.

"But long enough for him to convince himself he's taken everything he can from her mind," Ram corrected.

Counce gave a shrug. "Two weeks should be quite long enough. After that, when Bassett finds out he still hasn't got what he wanted, he may grow desperate and permanently injure the girl's mind. And if we let that happen, we'd never forgive ourselves."

"Have you decided yet how we're going to rescue her?" Falconetta inquired.

"Just grab her. By transfax."

"And make it obvious that we had a hand in it?" Ram objected. "After all, Bassett would recognize that a matter transmitter had been used."

"That's all to the good. When Bassett realizes that we are in such a strong position that we can give him information he thought would suffice, and he finds he has been hitting his head against a brick wall of our design, he's that much more likely to give way in sheer fury."

Ram hesitated. "It sounds logical," he conceded. "All right, we can try. We can only do our best, after all, and we're certainly doing that."

"I'd feel a hell of a sight more confident if we *weren't* already doing our best," snapped Counce. He dropped into a relaxer which stood close by, and wiped his hand across his eyes as though to rub away tiredness.

"I hate this blackmail," he said. "That's what it is, you know. With an admixture of bribery. Still, it's all we've got."

"I think you can dignify *our* contribution with a better name," Ram said gently. "Have you had a chance to watch the Falconetta Show lately?"

"No, but I expect that, as usual, half the population of Earth has been tuning in. What are you doing?"

"A series on the effects of intolerance in the history of pre-space Earth. There's a fad for the period at present. We contrast such affairs as the apartheid situation in

Africa and the persecution of the Australian aborigines with the advantages of co-operation. We shall climax with a hypothetical program regarding contact with intelligent aliens."

"It sounds valuable." Counce displayed sudden interest.

"For what it's worth," Falconetta qualified cynically. "We have the biggest audience on Earth, but we still only have it an hour a week, and the rest of the time the public is being fed the standard complacent pap. Damn it, Saïd, I sometimes think we could give the people the transfax and they would just put it in the corner with a dust-cover over it and bury their heads again. How the hell are we going to make people fit to live with intelligent aliens if they are still prepared to dislike human beings just because they were born under a different sun?"

"We're trying," Counce said wearily. "We are trying."

"But there remains the risk," Ram pointed out, "that even if we succeed in making our race fit to live with the Others, the Others may not be fit to live with us."

There were plans to deal with that, too; they thought in silence about the results of delivering fusion bombs by transfax into every major alien city.

The transfax alarm interrupted the pause. Counce opened the cabinet and found a single sheet of paper on its floor. He scanned it without expression.

"Do you remember we were discussing the most disastrous things that could happen to us?" he said at last. "Ram, you recall what you said?"

The old man nodded, clenching his thin hands to stop them from trembling.

"Well, it's happened. This is from Wu, on Regis. They've detected an alien ship. And it's been to Ymir.

They haven't heard from Jaroslav, but there isn't any room for doubt.

"We've been discovered, and all the careful work we've been doing to prepare for the event is still unfinished."

He sounded as if he was pronouncing an epitaph on mankind. He felt that quite possibly he was.

CHAPTER XI

THE COURSE was a true geodesic of the continuum — a straight line in the sense of being the actual shortest distance between two points — and that was suspicious in itself. For it implied the ship's crew knew what they were going to find.

Usually, a long voyage of exploration took the form of a series of dog-legs, from system to system; this one had bypassed half a dozen ostensibly promising stars, arrowing direct for Ymir's own sun.

The Others knew something.

Because of the lapse of time involved in the propagation of the betraying "wake" of a hyperphotonic vessel, the watchers on Regis did not know what was happening until the alien craft had already been to Ymir. It had spent a few days in the neighborhood — by a convenient miracle, at a time when no human-built spaceships were scheduled to call. It was a bare outside chance, then, that the Others might have the impression they had chanced across an indigenous life-form, rather than a colony planted from elsewhere. If they had observed reasonably closely during their brief stay, however, the chance would have diminished to vanishing point. It was not worth banking on.

Like it or not, they had to recognize that the human race's one advantage over the Others — that they knew of their competitors' existence — had been canceled out.

The news was broached by Katya Ivanovna, on duty in the ever-watchful detector room, where by turns every individual on Regis calculated, identified, and plotted the course of ships in space, both human and alien. Katya was that much faster than most of the group at reducing the pattern of the vibrations in the cosmos to a line on a three-dimensional graph. This time, she wasted the small advantage in checking her calculations for error, hoping against hope she might be wrong.

But the figures she gave to Wu left no room for doubt.

For a long time the director of the expedition sat silent at his desk, contemplating the neat handwritten symbols before him. At length he pushed his chair back and stood up.

"Well, we're on the downgrade now," he said. "So far as I can see at the moment, there's not a thing we can do. But we'll scrape the barrel for ideas just in case. Pass this news to *everybody*. Tell them to drop what they're doing and come here at once. Maybe someone will think of something."

"And if they don't?" Katya sounded as though she knew the answer to that; Wu gave it to her regardless.

"Then I guess we just have to blow them to bits."

He crossed the room to the master public-address panel and leaned his thumb heavily on the activating switch.

"Drop what you're doing, everybody, and come out into the plaza. The Others appear to have discovered Ymir. Somehow we've got to figure out a way of getting around this."

It was a dispirited group that assembled on the

hardbeaten sand of the plaza. Regis Main Base consisted of a haphazard arrangement of huts surrounding the heavy-duty transfax which was capable of handling practically any mass or size that might conceivably be required. They had chosen this spot for their base because it never rained, very seldom clouded over to interfere with local visual observation. The choice had drawbacks; one was that the heat was usually scorching around noon. People sweated and blinked their eyes as they waited for Wu to climb on the transfax platform and address them.

Miserably, Anty Dreean watched the director's compact figure rise to the impromptu dais, straighten, and look around. What the hell *could* be done? They might as well throw their hands in and go home — if they had any home to go to. Once you accepted the responsibility of the knowledge the group guarded, though, the group became your family. It had to. The risks were too great otherwise.

Now Wu picked up a hand amplifier and started to speak.

"We've detected the wake of an alien ship," he said baldly. "It apparently went straight from one of the Others' local bases to the Ymiran system. It spent a short time in scouting around. Now it's heading directly back the way it came. There's no room for doubt that we've been discovered; from what we know of the Others' preferences in regard to climate and atmosphere, they will automatically have decided we represent a serious rival to their ambitions. Ymir has always been a major threat in two respects; first, it is the nearest of the human-inhabited worlds, except for Regis, to the Others' sphere of activity; second, it is the only human-inhabited world which the Others could comfortably occupy.

"So far, presumably, none of the aliens except those actually aboard the scouting vessel are aware of our existence. I've seen figures on the ship's course. It is now about one day out from Ymir, and six to seven days from its home base. It will pass closest to Regis about two and a quarter days from now. We could transfax a bomb over such a distance and destroy it and the knowledge it carries.

"Only the fact that it went straight from its base to Ymir suggests that the Others decided the existence of a plane suitable for their race in that system. If their ship simply disappears without trace, they will send another; if they lose that too, they are probably sufficiently like ourselves in their patterns of thought to suspect deliberate interference. This problem presents the toughest enigma I can recall. We have less than two days in which to solve it some other way than by destroying the ship. Have you any suggestions?"

He looked around the gathering. He saw only downcast eyes, blank, worried expressions. The gloom was tangible, almost; everyone reflected that the aims they had given their lives to now stood in immediate danger of annihilation.

Anty Dreean felt perhaps the most miserable of all. He had not yet managed to grow accustomed to seeing his cherished intentions founder on a rock of hard fact. Like everyone else engaged in the vast plan—the plan to ensure that man and alien should profit and not suffer from their impending contact — he had given up everything to this single end. Failure was not simple failure; it was ultimate disaster.

Wu was speaking again. "We don't have to have a complete solution. A stopgap, first. You know that we are in sight of success if only we can have enough time. Saïd Counce is achieving wonders with his attempts to influence Bassett; Jaroslav Dubin is laying the foundation for implementing our plans on Ymir. If we can stave off contact for a few years more, we shall be able to risk cutting corners. At the moment, we daren't. Unless someone can suggest a means of gaining time, we shall be forced to sacrifice our entire hopes."

To his own complete astonishment, Anty Dreean found that he had an idea. He looked covertly round at his neighbors; their faces were as blank as before. He looked beyond, feeling afraid to speak out at once in case someone forestalled him with a better plan. No one spoke, and Wu shrugged and started to get down from the platform.

"Dr. Wu!" said Anty. "Just a moment, please."

Wu paused and looked round. "Yes, Anty?" he said. He didn't sound hopeful.

"We don't have to destroy the ship, you know," Anty ventured, and people everywhere in the plaza turned and looked at him. Self-consciously, he plunged ahead.

"We could kidnap it, couldn't we? And fake it to look as if the crew caught some dangerous disease on this planet they visited? After all, the people at their base don't know they didn't actually land on Ymir."

Wu gave a slow, thoughtful nod. "Anty, it just might be done. Someone give me a breakdown on power requirements."

"Fantastic!" snapped an anonymous voice from near the transfax platform. "You mean reach out across — what is it, eight parsecs? — and grab a large ship in full flight, and haul it clear back to Regis? It'd take ten to the tenth ergs per gram, or something like that. Ridiculous!"

"Not at all," contradicted someone else. "What we do is help ourselves to a hundred cubic yards of raw plasma out of the local sun, bottle it in a force field, and use that as a power source."

"Is that practical?" Wu glanced at the speaker.

"No. But it could be done if we had to do it," the man answered cynically.

Ideas bubbled up now like a hot spring through broken rocks; arguments started at a dozen points in the plaza as to the feasibility of the idea. Slide rules and calculators were already being applied to the mathematical questions involved.

"Dr. Wu," someone called out. "What exactly do we do with the ship once we've got it?" That same question must have been in a hundred minds, for there was a chorus of agreement.

"Anty?" said Wu, looking down. "Could you enlarge on that point?"

"I was thinking we could bring the ship down near the pole, where the Others landed before. Then we could get the crew out and make non-living duplicates of them, and fill them full of some mutated culture of a native Ymiran microorganism."

"Could we do it in time?" objected yet another voice, a chorus from a group of biochemists assured him they would do their damnedest.

"That's all very fine and large! That means we have to put the ship right back on its original course afterwards, with its dummy crew of corpses," the same voice snapped; and the technicians who had furiously been calculating power requirements immediately doubled their original estimates and frowned over the result.

"All right! All right!" Wu shouted into his hand amplifier; silence fell like tropical night. "We'll have to look into this in detail. Break it up and get on with it. The moment the ship comes within range, we want to seize it and 'fax it here to Regis. We have to deal with the crew before the ship theoretically gets out of range again, so that we can put it back where it would have got to if we hadn't interfered. You've got one hour to tell me whether or not it can be done!"

The group dispersed quickly, leaving Anty Dreean standing rather foolishly by himself twenty paces from the transfax platform. Wu set down his hand amplifier and looked the young man up and down.

"Thank you, Anty," he said in a voice that barely carried across the gap. "I think you've solved it."

Anty tried to appear modest. He felt completely overwhelmed.

"If it can be made to work," Wu continued, "you realize what it means, don't you?"

"A breathing space," said Anty, puzzled.

"I mean for yourself." Wu was measuring his words. "It means that we shall really have to start taking notice of you, Anty. It looks to me as though you've got what Saïd Counce has — the talent we need most desperately. The ability to stand a problem on its head, so that it loses its difficulty. It isn't a conscious talent. It's just a gift. I thought it would be better to warn you. Because if you *have* got it, your life is going to be hell from here on out, with people pestering you night and day to give them the answers they can't get themselves. You'd better have a talk with Saïd, young man, and let him warn you himself."

He got down from the platform and walked across to where Anty stood. "You'll get the dirtiest jobs of all, Anty. I can only hope you'll enjoy it."

The director's seriousness made Anty uncomfortable. He said, "Well, we don't know yet if it'll work or not. What can I do towards finding out? Everyone seems to be working on *something*."

"Go and poke your nose in," said Wu. "I mean it. Just go and poke your nose in. Find out why people think it won't work, and tell them why it will. Damn it, it's your plan! You go *make* it work!"

CHAPTER XII

A LITTLE TIMIDLY, Anty obeyed. Wu, with a parting nod, more perhaps of commiseration than commendation, had turned his back and walked away across the plaza to his own office. At random, Anty cast around for a place to begin; he chose a hut which proved to be full of a babel of shouted calculations.

"Anty!" someone cried as he opened the door. "Is this list of power requirements complete now?" A paper was thrust under Anty's nose; he took it and tried to organize his racing thoughts enough to answer the question.

"Uh — you haven't taken account of the need to duplicate the alien crew," he ventured. "And won't we have to keep our own transfax running continuously to bring stuff in from off-world?"

The compiler of the list snatched it back. "Don't need to worry about that; we just keep ours idling and use the power available at the delivery end to get the stuff through. But you're right about the duplication business, damn it. Anyone got any idea of the mass of one of these Others?"

"Better allow a hundred kilos," suggested a girl running a manual computer, not interrupting the play of her fingers over its keyboard.

"Yes, but how many times over? Damn it, we'll guess at twenty. If there are more, we can leave it to their imagination to guess that the others died and were buried on Ymir. What's the average molecular weight of their protoplasm?" he added, trying to set a slide rule and talk at the same time.

"Bio would know," the girl answered.

"I'm going that way," offered Anty. "I'll get them to call through with the data."

The biochemists were huddled over a heap of cell charts; on a huge wallboard someone had already sketched a tentative mutation for an Ymiran microorganism which might convincingly infect the Others. "Anty!" said one of them as the door opened. "How the hell are we going to get a decent-sized sample of Ymiran germs? There aren't any culture plants on Ymir."

"Well —" Anty fumbled. "Wouldn't Jaroslav be carrying some of the adaptable ones in his own mucous membranes when he came through?"

"Anty, you're a genius," the speaker replied. "If they can adapt to the warm environment of a human being — and we know some of them can — those are the ones we need to work with. Is Jaroslav coming?"

"If he doesn't, he'll be the only one," someone replied absently.

"The technical section wants to know what the average molecular weight of the Others' protoplasm is," Anty said. The remark produced a dead silence for fifteen seconds.

"*Average?*" echoed a man whose hands were delicately shaping a chromosome-structure analogue out of odd lengths of grooved plastic. "They're the mathematical wizards; we'll send them the total and tell them to work out the average themselves."

"I guess that'll do," Anty agreed.

In the logistics section, as soon as the door opened to admit Anty, no less than three people yelled for his attention. The logistical question would be the toughest of all; it was no use being able to handle all the individual parts of the job unless they could be handled simultaneously and in the right order.

"What's all this about?"

"Now look, you can't expect —"

"There isn't a hope of —"

Puzzled at their seeming obtuseness, Anty patiently explained what all this was about, why he did expect, and that there was not only a hope but a certainty of. He left that hut with a slight feeling of bafflement. Now that he had a chance to think over the details, he was more and more convinced that his inspiration was workable. If he could demolish all the objections to it as easily as those last three, there was no doubt it would come off perfectly.

Only that again turned on one crucial point. He went to the detector room to check on it.

Katya Ivanovna was alone in the midst of the glowing signal lights, the quavering dials, the faintly humming apparatus. She did not look up as Anty came quietly in, but she greeted him in a gentle voice.

"Wait a moment, Anty. I've just got to establish this limit beyond question."

Obediently, Anty remained silent near the door, looking at the equipment, wondering what it was going to tell them. Katya worked over her calculations, breathing heavily, occasionally muttering a quiet curse as something turned out unfavorably. At length she sighed and sat back in her chair.

"We can do it, Anty," she said. "We can really do it. The power experts gave me their estimate five minutes ago, and I've just been reading off on the dials. We can we can keep it for a day and a half at least before we have to put it back where it came from. Assuming nothing goes wrong, of course."

She rustled papers together and swung her chair to face him.

"Congratulations!"

Anty avoided her gaze. "It doesn't seem to me that I've done anything much," he muttered, acutely aware of the lack of experience and the youth which he still bore with him.

"Nothing much, hey? We'll see. Don't let it worry you if you get a bit swollen-headed watching us go to work on your brilliant scheme. It's going to be impressive." She glanced at her watch. "Suppose we step into the plaza? I think it's going to begin."

"Already?" said Anty, astonished. "But you only just finished your calculations!"

Katya grinned. "You don't think Wu would let a little thing like practicability stand in the way, do you? We've been ordering people to come here for more than half an hour."

Through the windows of the hut, the glare from outside suddenly redoubled in intensity. "There goes the transfax," Katya said. "Dark glasses, young man — quick, or we'll miss the start of it."

It was spectacular, not merely impressive. The three agents from Wu's home world of K'ung-fu-tse were the first to arrive. They came straight through the transfax field in rockets, which soared vertically upwards, looped, circled and were already on their way to a landing when the next batch arrived.

"Verity!" called Katya to a white-haired woman sitting

astride a sort of monstrous mechanical horse, which tugged a trailer-load of electrical equipment out of the transfax field. "What the deuce have you got there?"

"I pinched a complete broadcast power-unit off a new construction project," Verity called back cheerfully. "I thought it would come in handy." Catching sight of Anty, she gave a wild wave before lumbering off across the plaza with her vast vehicle.

After that people and equipment seemed to come in equal quantities. Counce came through from Earth, bringing nothing but his unparalleled experience. Then from Shiva; then from Zeus; then from New Peru; then more from Earth.

Watching, Anty felt a chill of sheer awe race down his spine. This was the organization to which he belonged to, to which he had given his life. An organization dedicated to a dream and a vision — without rules, except those they imposed on themselves, without any qualification for membership except the desire to serve one's fellow man.

Like an army going into battle, they were assembling here from every world occupied by man, but especially from the mother-world of Earth. Those from the colder worlds stopped only to discard their outer clothing as they emerged into the blazing heat of Regis; those from tropical climates did not even waste that much time before going to work.

First, the transfax units — one to seize the raw plasma out of the sun; another (because the first would be totally destroyed by the fantastic heat) to reach across the parsecs and kidnap the alien ship. That one they sent up to the polar regions. It seemed that it had barely gone from sight before one of the rockets from K'ung-fu-tse took off awkwardly for the weight of a drum of power cable under its starboard wing and began to lay a snakelike thread of it across the landscape. A second followed it. That would be enough to convey the incredible flow of power for the few vital seconds.

Men and women had scrambled into spacesuits; now the main transfax was temporarily withdrawn from import duty and used to hurl a duplicate of itself, an assembly crew, and the complete broadcast power-unit Verity had brought from Boreas into orbit far overhead. When they seized the plasma from the sun, they would have to use the vacuum of space itself to insulate it, draw off its power on the spot, and broadcast it to ground in a tight beam.

Power cables spread over the base, like the web of a crazy spider; jury-rigged scaffolding canted upwards, carrying the power unit subassemblies. But there was more going on than could be plainly seen. In one of the huts Jaroslav was being deprived of a colony of involuntary fellow-travelers — germs native to Ymir, which were slapped into cold-culture dishes and used as the basis for the artificial "disease" the Others were to carry home with them. Far to the north, a team of men and women sweated and slaved to prepare the transfax for receiving the ship.

The sun went down; came up again. It still looked on a frantic hive of activity, but there was order where there had been chaos. Technicians were running preliminary tests now; there was time to snatch a bite to eat and a glass of water. Red-eyed with fatigue, Anty Dreean walked slowly through the midst of it all, wondering at his inspiration become reality.

"Anty!" said a familiar voice, and he turned to see Counce waving to him. A little shyly, because Counce was a great man, Anty returned the greeting.

"Good," Counce said briefly, and made a gesture that took in the entire scene. There was no need to say more;

Anty went on his way feeling that he had received an accolade.

A small group was emerging from Wu's office: Wu himself, Katya, a woman so beautiful she could only be Falconetta, and a white-haired old man. Katya waved and called to Anty, who hurried across to them. They were engaged in frantic discussion.

"So you're Anty Dreean," said the very beautiful woman, giving him a smile that made him very much aware of his youthful susceptibility. "This is a fine idea you had, but there seems to be one thing you overlooked completely. What are we going to do with the aliens when we've got them out of their ship? Leave them to their own devices?"

"Why —" began Anty, and Katya interrupted.

"That's unfair of you, Falconetta! Don't worry, Anty. We have it in hand. This is Ram Singh, one of our greatest psychologists — the man who's re-educating the people of Earth single-handed."

The old man chuckled. "Trying to, and finding it hard. What we have to do, Anty, is to convince the Others that we intend them no harm. This will call for acting — communication in symbols. I produce television broadcasts, and I know quite a lot about communicating that way. So we shall see what we can do. First, though, we have to get the Others to Regis, and that's the most important part."

He glanced round at Wu, who nodded. "And we're just about ready to do that now," he said.

A technician gave a final check to the power-beam receiver and nodded with satisfaction. The transfax died into inactivity; everywhere men and women started to withdraw to their posts.

Taking up his hand amplifier, Wu went to the transfax platform and climbed up to survey the scene. Everywhere he looked, men and women signaled readiness. He licked his lips. Anty felt a sudden tightness grip his belly. Now?

"Now!" said Wu, and his voice boomed through the amplifier. For an age-long instant, nothing seemed to happen; then Anty felt a touch on his arm. It was Falconetta.

"Look up there!" she said, pointing, and he looked. Overhead, so bright that it shone through the blue sky like a new star, gleamed a point of light: sun-stuff, ripped by men from its home to serve them in their hour of desperate need.

CHAPTER XIII

THE WHOLE gigantic task, which had taken so many people so many hours to plan, lasted less than a fraction of a second.

First, they stole the plasma from the sun; the transfax which had seized it boiled instantly into nothing, or rather into insignificant, contaminating gases. They were ready to trap it in insubstantial but invulnerable bands of magnetic force, a tiny star from which they could drain the power they wanted.

This power they flashed to the ground below, in a beam so tight even the air through which it passed barely diminished its intensity. A receiver stood the shock for moments only, feeding the power into the cables which had been laid at rocket-speed across the face of the planet. The metal skeleton of the receiver glowed, burned although it was made of steel, stood out on the retinas of the watchers in vivid silhouette-like afterimages.

The cables burned too, sizzling across the horizon like a twofold train of gunpowder ignited with a match. Black oily smoke from the insulation drifted lazily in the light wind after the current had passed.

And in the cold arctic night, a group of silent people saw

materialized before their eyes a ship that had not been built by human hands.

They had not calculated exactly right; the mass of the vessel was too great, and instead of dropping to rest on the area prepared for it, it sprawled across the transfax platform and crushed it to smithereens. There would be another ready by the time they had to send the vessel back. No one had time to worry about such small points as these; the main thing, the only thing, was that their incredible gamble had paid off.

For a long moment there was no reaction; then the tension dissolved into jubilation, and they clapped one another on the back and laughed out of sheer relief. Someone remembered to radio Main Base with the good news, and warn them that the transfax receiver up here was smashed.

When Wu received the message, he clambered down from the platform and gave Anty a thoughtful look. "Well, I warned you," he said. "It's gone off perfectly so far."

"What's this about?" demanded Falconetta, and Wu wryly repeated the warning he had earlier given to Anty.

"I don't think Saïd finds his work unpleasant," Falconetta commented. "But I'll ask him sometime. Anty, is there any way of getting up to the north now the transfax is out there?"

"I'll check," said Anty obligingly, automatically dropping back into his accustomed role of newest recruit and errand boy. When he had hurried off, Ram Singh raised one fine white eyebrow at his companion.

"You had a reason for that," he said. "You know perfectly well that whether or not the transfax is functioning at the polar base we can still be sent there with a little extra power. If Anty had thought for a moment or two, he would have seen that fact himself."

Falconetta did not reply directly; instead, she looked at Wu. "That's a nice boy you have there, Wu," she said. "Why are you being unkind to him? Is it because you're jealous?"

"Jealous? I suppose I am. I haven't tried to do more than give him a fair appraisal of the problems facing him, though."

"If he's as capable as he seems, he'll figure them out for himself." Falconetta turned her smoky-yellow eyes speculatively after Anty. "He reminds me more than a little of myself, when I was new. He is an original, isn't he?"

"Yes, that's his born self."

Anty was returning, and called out when he was still a dozen paces distant. "They're warming up the transfax now for us to get to the northern base. They're passing out protective clothing at the stores hut; I think we'd better get some and go right away."

A few minutes later they walked through onto the bare, frosty ground, and saw the alien ship lying like a stranded whale under the harsh floodlights. They were only a short distance from the site of the excavation that had revealed the traces of the Others' first visit to Regis, and Anty found himself contrasting the circumstances of the two ships' arrivals. What would the reaction be of the inhuman minds in the enigmatic, almost featureless hull? What were they thinking? Had they any idea where they were? Perhaps they could tell from the star patterns, if the first ship that called here had made a record of them and passed it on.

They waited while Wu made a circuit of the perimeter. A battery of floodlights illuminated each side of the ship, concentrating on the barely visible outline of the airlocks. The vessel itself was not unlike a human ship; after all, it was built to the same physical laws, driven by similar methods — there had to be some identity. Yet there was a difference, and Anty found his pulse quickening as it had done when he dug up the alien-made cathode-ray tube from the permafrozen ground.

Now, at last, the long-awaited moment of contact between the races was at hand. And thanks to his own idea, it was man who would dictate the circumstances. Ironical, that when they had devoted so much work to the cause they believed in — that man and alien should live in peace — when it came to this point they did not dare trust the aliens to act of their own accord.

Ram and Falconetta were discussing in low tones their project for making their peaceful intentions known to the Others. Anty wanted desperately to eavesdrop, but respected their obviously deliberate whispering.

Satisfied, Wu returned from his tour. "Well?" he said, addressing Ram. "Made your mind up?"

The old man inclined his white head. "I think so," he answered. "We are agreed that it will be best to wait for some action by the aliens before we ourselves make any move. They will require some time to adjust to what has happened."

"As you will," conceded Wu. "In that case, I'll reduce the watch to a rota, and give people a chance to go back to Main Base and rest and relax."

He glanced at Anty. "How about you? You must be pretty well exhausted by now."

"I think I'd prefer to stay and see what happens," Anty ventured.

"I think he deserves to," Falconetta put in, and Wu, after an instant's hesitation, nodded and walked away.

But nothing did happen. Nothing at all.

As the hours ticked away, the biochemists began to

worry about their carefully prepared cultures; the technicians began to wonder whether they would have time enough to duplicate the crew and plant the dummies aboard the ship, the men and women in the logistics section worried about getting the alien supplies out of the ship to provision the real crew members while they were stranded here on Regis. And Katya, in the detector hut back at Main Base, watched the line indicating the limit of their available power converge on the line indicating the theoretical course of the ship.

Six hours went by.

Wu called a hasty conference in the lee of an outcrop of rock, and Ram, Falconetta, Counce, Anty and two or three others stood shivering while they talked the situation over.

"As we see it, then," Wu summed up, "one of two things must have happened. Either the shock of what has happened has stunned the crew into complete inactivity, which we regard as unlikely — or something has harmed them, some unlooked-for consequence of the 'faxing of their ship to Regis. We daren't wait any longer for them to make a move. We shall have to move ourselves. What do we do?"

"Find out by direct inspection," said Anty bluntly. He was more confident about speaking up now; everywhere, since his inspiration had paid off, he found his companions regarding him with new respect and no longer any hint of patronage.

"Explain," commanded Wu.

Anty shrugged. "Put someone aboard the ship by transfax. I'd very much like to go myself."

The others exchanged glances. "There doesn't seem to be any alternative," conceded Counce. He spoke for them all; the decision was taken.

Heart pounding, breath rasping in his throat, Anty opened his eyes. They had scanned the hull of the ship with sonar detectors, seeking an open space or compartment within. One near the stern, which gave echoes consistent with a partly-empty storage room, had been selected — and here he was. He had materialized a foot above the floor, so that he would have air to push aside, and not find himself partly embedded in a solid object. That sort of mistake resulted in explosions.

The thud as he dropped to the floor seemed to fill the universe; automatically Anty crouched into a corner and waited for fear one of the Others might have heard him arrive. He remained frozen for long minutes, studying his surroundings by the beam of a powerful flashlight.

Good guessing; this was indeed a storeroom, its walls lined with shelves and the shelves filled with flat, square containers stacked together. The shock of landing on Regis had scattered some of the neat piles and tipped them to the floor. When he rose from his cramped hiding place he had to walk carefully to avoid treading on them.

The door of the room opened easily once he had solved the mystery of its alien fastening. He slid it back in smooth-running grooves, and looked both ways along a corridor beyond. The alien lamps were redder than those used by humans; that was natural enough. They favored worlds with redder suns.

Cautiously, he ventured out into the passage and began to tiptoe towards the bow. The air was perfectly breathable — the Others liked roughly the same concentration of oxygen as did human beings. But it was cold, and vague but definite smells assailed his nose. Alien smells. Hints of ammonia, sulphur, other less definable odors.

A few yards ahead of him, there was an intersection.

He was approaching it gingerly when a clattering noise made him draw back. Across the intersection hastened one of the blocky aliens, carrying indeterminate objects; he — or possibly she — was in such a hurry that he failed to spot Anty crouching in the shadows.

So they were neither in coma through psychological shocks, nor rendered incapable of action by physical damage. What, then, could be the reason for their absolute quiescence?

A sudden ring of brightness, crossed by shadows, struck down the right-hand passage from the direction in which the alien had gone. At the same time, a cool breeze could be felt. They had opened an airlock, then. At last they were coming out!

Vaguely disappointed that he would not after all be the first human being to confront an alien face to — to whatever the Others had to correspond to a face, Anty remained where he was.

A sharp report rang out. Another. Then there were bass-voiced, inhuman cries, and several more aliens ran across the intersection. This time Anty could see what the things were they carried. They were long tubes mounted on handles, with racks of blunt-nosed cylindrical objects attached at the side.

They were guns!

He started forward with a despairing cry, and came to the intersection. Looking towards the airlocks, he saw the Others piling out, wriggling past one of their number who was sighting his gun on an unseen target. He fired, and gave a grunt of triumph.

Then, attracted perhaps by Anty's movements, he glanced down. Before Anty could say or do anything, the Other recognized him, dragged his weapon back over the rim of the airlock, and fired.

There was a vast pain in Anty's chest. Something was dragging him off balance. A terrible weakness overcame him.

The last thing he saw before his eyes failed was redness glowing beyond the airlock, and the last thing he heard was the noise of the three rockets from K'ung-fu-tse, which had been patrolling overhead, as they swooped down howling toward the alien ship.

After that he knew nothing.

CHAPTER XIV

"I SIMPLY didn't know it was possible to feel so depressed," said Wu bluntly. Counce nodded, and gave a cursory glance around the perimeter of the site. It was like a battlefield. It *was* a battlefield.

Filthy, sweat-damp, hands covered with mud, the two men stood beside one of the still-functioning batteries of arc lights. The aliens had managed to shoot four of them out with their first burst, but the survivors, redistributed, were adequate for the work in progress.

"Not exactly a promising augury for future contacts, is it?" Counce said. "Anybody find out what happened to Anty?"

"I sent someone into the ship to bring out his body," Wu answered.

"A pity, that. Still, he's the tough kind — it shouldn't do him any permanent harm." Counce made as though to wipe his face with the back of his hand, saw the layer of crusted dirt on his skin, and changed his mind. "How many of us did they get altogether?"

"Eighteen dead. There are several seriously wounded — the medics are deciding now whether they'll heal or whether they would do better to finish them and let them start again. I still haven't pieced together a coherent picture of what happened."

"It looked quite clear from where I was standing," Counce declared. "They opened the airlocks simultaneously and shot out as many of the lights as they could; then a gunner at each lock covered for his companions as they piled out. It looks to me as if their commander gave them some guff about selling their lives dearly. Well, they did that all right."

"I'd give my right hand to know why they were so sure we were hostile," muttered Wu.

The party that had gone into the alien ship was starting to return; they handed Anty's body down from the lock and two of their number half-carried, half-dragged it to the perimeter. After that they began to bring out the aliens' supplies, and the other equipment that they might need.

"The poor bastards," Wu said after a pause. "I hated to do what we did."

"Well, we couldn't just sit around and let them massacre us," Counce snapped. "From the way this lot behaved, I get the impression they are slightly less than trustworthy. How many survivors were there in the end?"

"Just the one — a young male. I had him put over yonder in a tent, and they're working on his injuries. I had a couple of computer experts assigned to build a language converter for him. By now they should have established the basics, if he's co-operating at all."

"So what are you thinking of doing about the ship?"

"We'll put the corpses back aboard, after mutilating them a bit more; then I propose to 'fax a hunk of Ymiran rock into the engine room, and we'll put it back on its original course. Let them worry about it. We haven't got time for anything more elaborate."

A voice hailed him through a hand amplifier from the far

side of the perimeter; he excused himself, and went to see what was wrong. Counce remained gloomily by himself under the glaring lights.

It was not a happy augury, this meeting. They had been perhaps overready to assume that the Others were prepared to meet mankind; on the recent showing, man was infinitely better fitted for the contact than the aliens were.

He sighed. From now on, therefore, they would have to devote still more of their exiguous resources to purely defensive matters; they would always have to be ready to kidnap alien ships, confuse the issue, muddle the Others and so stop them from realizing the truth.

Around him the situation slowly crystallized into action. They slammed the hunk of rock into the delicate mechanism of the engine room, producing a shattering explosion. The alien corpses would be battered past recognition; only the unkindest chance would reveal that death was actually due to the hot blast of rocket motors and not to accident. A quick operation with the transfax ripped a piece of the hull away; if they counted the dead bodies and found one short, that rip would explain the missing crewman.

Again they set up the power transmitters, again the racing rockets laid their trails of cable; again the plasma bloomed like a tiny star in orbit overhead. And the alien ship was gone with its cargo of death. Let the Others make of the mystery what they would; time was too short to tie up all the loose ends.

Counce's every limb ached; his eyes were red with fatigue. He took a deep breath and drilled himself back towards action. There was the survivor, over yonder in a lighted tent. On that single survivor now depended whether or not the human race could persuade the aliens to accept and trust them.

The tent was a large one. In the center, under a reddish light suited to his organs of vision, the captive lay on a couch which had been taken from the ship. As he entered, Counce reflected on the creature's appearance, which was neither ugly nor attractive by human standards; solid, thick-set, in a way, neutral. He wondered whether by some mischance he himself and other human beings might appear loathsome to the Others.

"Good evening, Saïd," said the biologist working on the creature's gashed limbs, glancing up from his task. But Counce ignored the greeting.

"Who put these straps on?" he said in a tone like thunder. He flung out his right arm and pointed to thick bands encircling the alien's limbs, fastening them to the couch.

"We had to," the biologist explained defensively. "He wouldn't hold still for us to dress his wounds."

"You must be out of your mind," said Counce wearily, and thrust the man aside as he bent to undo the bonds.

"All right," he said, standing back. "Get on with what you were doing."

Apprehensively, the man started to obey; at a sudden movement from the captive, he drew back, flinching. "Get on with it, idiot!" Counce ordered. "By this time he must know you're trying to help."

The alien's flat-eyed face watched them warily; Counce wondered what he would have been thinking in a similar position, and then realized there was no comparison. He would have had a hope to buoy him up—the hope of fruitful intercourse between the races. This alien was young, and probably had fully accepted the word of his superiors aboard the ship that men could only be enemies. There were painted symbols on his hard gray hide — what did they mean? An answer to that would have to wait.

But one small victory had been won; it seemed that the movement which had so startled the biologist had been intended only to present the injured limb more conveniently to his hands. Satisfied that the job was going smoothly now, Counce turned to the language technicians working on their converter at the back of the tent.

"How's it going?" he demanded.

The nearer technician — a girl — raised her head, and Counce recognized her as one of Ram's staff from Video India. "It isn't going," she said bluntly. "We know they use speech because we heard them during the fight, but since he came in here he hasn't uttered a sound."

"Do what you can anyway," Counce answered, and with a final glance around he left the tent.

It was no use; he was exhausted, and he knew it. Even if the biologist's action in strapping the alien down had been criminally thoughtless, he had been wrong in snapping at the man as he had. He needed sleep, and he needed it now.

In the shelter of a pile of miscellaneous crates and boxes, he found a discarded heap of protective clothing stripped from the eighteen who had died victims of alien bullets. Here, he decided, would do as well as anywhere; he threw himself down and was almost instantly asleep.

It was still dark when Counce awoke; Regis's polar night was not yet past its middle. Hungry, but fantastically refreshed by his slumber, he got to his feet and went in search of news of what had passed.

The scene had changed again, radically; except for the tent where the alien lay, the site was deserted. Everyone would have gone back to base, of course; there was much to be done. Probably people would be hunting for him there. He saw that an emergency transfax unit had been left behind near the alien's tent, and he made towards it.

As he neared it, however, it burst into life, and someone stepped through from beyond. The sudden light dazzled him, and he shaded his eyes in an attempt to make out who the new arrival might be.

"Saïd!" exclaimed a familiar voice. It was Falconetta, nearly unrecognizable in the thick garments shrouding her slim body. "Are you all right?"

"Of course I am," Counce answered, and explained briefly what had happened. "What's going on at base?"

"Mainly, we're replacing the casualties. Ram had to go back to Earth, but I said I'd stay to see what was being done about the alien. Do you know?"

"I haven't had the chance to ask since I woke up. He's over in that tent."

Falconetta's reply was to head briskly in that direction, and Counce automatically followed.

In the tent, the alien lay still, warily, watchfully studying his captors. The biologist had gone, to be replaced by a young man in a brown cloak; the two language experts were dozing over their computer, and three young men who had brought in a pile of alien supplies and a bowl of melted ice — which was necessary, they knew, to the Other's metabolism — sat dispiritedly on chairs near the entrance.

"Not a thing," said one of the last three in reply to the newcomers' question. "He doesn't move except to stretch his limbs; he won't utter a sound, and he won't take food or water."

"How about the language converter?" Counce nodded at it.

"They tried him with all the possible basics. They didn't get a peep out of him."

"Sometimes I think we're capable of the most dreadful stupidity," Falconetta said suddenly. "Saïd, this poor creature probably thinks he's being guarded with all these people around. Clear them out of the tent, will you?"

"And leave you alone with this thing?" said the previous speaker in alarm. "You must be crazy!"

"What could he do to me except kill me?" Falconetta snapped. "Out, all of you!"

They looked at Counce; after a moments' pause, he nodded, and shook the language technicians into wakefulness. Bleary-eyed, bleary-minded, they raised no objection.

Outside under the winter stars they waited, shivering, wondering what was going on inside that tent. "Do you really reckon she knows what she's doing?" one of the group asked of the air.

"If anyone does, she does," Counce answered. They went on waiting.

And then the flap of the tent lifted. Limping, awkward, the alien came out, leaning his hugely solid body on Falconetta's small shoulder.

Declining offers of assistance with urgent gestures, she helped the alien to a nearby pile of boxes, where he transferred his weight to their support and looked around. What his thoughts were as he recognized the place where his ship had lain, and realized that he was indeed totally alone among members of another race, they could not tell. But that did not matter. For the moment it was only important that another victory had been won; one of the Others had accepted help from a human being, not once, but twice.

Counce gave Falconetta a smile which said more than a million words.

They were waiting in silence for the outcome, when the

transfax platform once more lit the landscape with its alarming brilliance, and a stranger walked, wild-eyed, into their midst. His face, his body, they had not seen before; he went unsteadily on his feet as though he had this moment learned to put them one before the other. After a few strides, he halted and looked at them, recognition dawning.

"Hello, Anty," said Falconetta softly.

CHAPTER XV

"SO FAR, NOT SO BAD," said Counce contentedly. As always at Main Base on Regis, the air was wonderfully warm; he could not think of it as sweltering hot after spending so long in the rigid arctic. "We really managed a breakthrough to the alien. His name is pretty well unpronounceable, but we found he could articulate the word 'friend,' so we're calling him that. It'll have advantageous psychological repercussions when they start to understand our language."

He wolfed another sandwich from the tray on Wu's desk, and sent a vast gulp of water after it.

"But the long-term question remains," said Katya; she sat on the far side of Wu's desk, legs crossed, head thrown back in a characteristic pose. "We have this one alien — what are we going to do with him? Keep him in isolation on Regis? We can't send him home, that's for sure."

"We shall have to appoint him a sort of ambassador," Wu suggested. "There's no alternative to keeping him on Regis until the time comes for further contact between the races; then, obviously, we shall have to ask him to go back to his own kind and tell them about us."

"We'll leave the details of that," Counce added. "Right now, we have a respite — maybe a long one, depending on how the Others react to getting their ship back with a dead crew and a wrecked engine room. In all probability they'll send another ship to Ymir right away. The fact that the first one went straight to the Ymiran system indicates they want to inspect that particular planet pretty badly. But the next time, we can be ready for them. There can't be any more off-the-cuff projects — they're very risky, even if this one worked."

"Anty Dreean doesn't seem to think it worked," said Katya delicately. "So far as he's concerned, the fact that the Others came out fighting means the idea was a complete flop."

"Some of his present depression is certainly due to shock," Wu interjected. "But in general it's disappointing that he should have reacted this way. It will take a long time to make him regain his confidence, and I was certain he was going to turn out to be a valuable ideas-man."

Counce swallowed the last sandwich on the tray and gave a parodied grin of satisfaction. "It won't be difficult," he said. "In fact, I already know how we're going to set him up in his own estimation again. I propose giving him a very responsible task in the near future, as soon as he's properly adjusted to his new body."

He selected his intonation carefully so that his hearers would take it for granted he had not yet chosen the task he proposed to set. They did so, and Wu changed the subject.

"We can't keep the Others away from Ymir indefinitely," he said. "Probably it will be a weight off our minds to know that we must now physically interfere with their attempts to go there. But it will give us correspondingly increased headaches trying to accelerate the process of stripping the planet clean for them. Saïd?" He acknowledged a questioning glance from Counce.

"May I be platitudinous for a moment and simply review our intentions?" Counce requested. "I think it often helps to get rid of details and see the outline again. It sometimes changes without our noticing.

"The real menace of Ymir, as we know, is due on the one hand to its being inhabited by people who are of the whole human race the least fitted to make harmonious contact with the Others, and on the other to its situation and its climate — which make it an obvious choice for the Others to colonize. The real solution, the one we are so confident Bassett will continue to overlook, depends on the fact that it is simply *not fit* for the human race.

"We agreed originally on combining the solutions to our problems. We need, first, to reconcile the various groups of the human race to differences among our own species, so that they will be more ready to tolerate alien intelligence, and, second, to give proof of our good will to the Others. We can achieve both by abandoning Ymir to them and scattering the ten million inhabitants throughout the rest of the galaxy. Ridicule will do the rest."

His listeners looked politely bored. "So?" said Katya bluntly.

"So be patient a moment longer. Now our own resources are too small and spread too thin for us to undertake this enormous job ourselves. Fortunately, Bassett — who can call on gigantic resources of man-power, technical ability and financial aid — was in one sense attacking the same problem. We are very near to success in making him desperate enough to enlist our help; I doubt whether it will be more than another few months before he goes to Video India and places the

111

order for the advertisement I told him to insert."

"That sounds good," approved Wu. "But —"

"So," Counce continued unperturbed, within the next few months, in addition to everything else, we have to reconcile the governments of all the inhabited worlds to accepting about a third of a million Ymirans each. Earth, of course, will present no problem — Bassett will see to that. But how do you think K'ung-fu-tse will react, for instance, Wu?"

The director rubbed his chin. "The question is rather academic. My world has a tradition of diligent hard work and in general is of a tolerant attitude. If the government were promised a third of a million hard-working, industrious immigrants, they would doubtless agree without hesitation. Bassett could not promise people like that from Earth — you Earthborn are too conditioned to long periods of leisure and high standards of comfort."

"Correct. That is one of Bassett's fundamental errors, of course. The way to persuade the outworld governments to fall in with his original scheme would have been to ask them initially to accept immigrants from similar worlds to their own, and not from Earth. Bassett, though, could not have provided them, so he doubtless overlooked that point."

"I feel heartened," said Katya with unexpected depth of feeling. "For the first time since we've started, I really have a conviction that we're going to succeed."

"At least," said Wu with an unaffected solemnity, "we can see answers of a sort to all our problems now."

They were stepping across the parsecs now, those who had come to Regis in answer to a cry of desperate need. They were used to answering such cries; indeed, they had given up their lives to answer the most despairing of all.

Some of them, like Anty Dreean, were young and idealistic; some, like Verity of Boreas, who had recruited Anty, and Ram Singh of Earth, were elderly. They too were idealists.

Back to their normal tasks as scientists, administrators, doctors, experts in a hundred different human disciplines, the loneliest and yet least lonely of all men and women were returning. Counce had to wait on line at the Main Base transfax and exchanged greetings with the others whom he had not had time to see and speak to during the past hectic hours.

But it was plain that he preferred silence, and after a word or two everyone respected his unspoken wish.

He was thinking partly of what they, but mostly of what he himself, had done.

Three hundred years, he thought. *That's a long time to wait to know if one was right . . .*

He knew now, though. He had seen the proof in the way the Others had come out of their ship into the polar winter of Regis, determined to sell their lives dearly to people who had no desire to buy them at any price. Had the situation been reversed, had the human beings present at this first contact not been convinced as they were of the need for tolerance and forbearance, there could have been a war, instead of a brief and bloody battle on a single planet.

In the last resort, no individual can trust any other individual, and yet without trust there can be no constructive effort, no co-operation. The Others had been unable to trust themselves to the strangers who had — seemingly without effort — dragged their ship across the star lanes; Counce himself had been unable to trust his fellow-men three hundred years before, and he had seen at the outset that he must learn to trust himself before he could call on them for help.

He remembered, as he stepped into the transfax and gave the identifying name of the receiver to which he wished to go, how he had sat by himself in that very distant past and looked up and down a certain table of mathematical symbols. They promised him — and mankind — two freedoms: one from the barrier of distance, the other from death itself.

At the time when he chanced across this particular application of hyperphotonic energy mechanics, the emigrations from Earth were just passing their peak. Earth had rid itself of its misfits, its outcasts, its social failures — and by a process of hard weeding-out, the colonies were adjusting towards stability.

The technique which was implicit in the details facing him would have turned that outburst into a true explosion, would have meant that men were free to step from world to world as easily as through a door. And there was more to it than that. Provided there was sufficient power, one could transmit anything from anywhere else to a suitable receiver; conversely, one could send anything — most importantly another transfax unit — anywhere distant. The galaxy suddenly seemed to close in on him like the walls of the room in which he was sitting.

Last, but very far from least, one could record whatever one transmitted, up to and including a living human being, and then re-create from the recording a facsimile of what had been sent.

Immortality — for the few.

Counce had sat at his table one whole night, thinking of the certainty which the laws of chance decreed: that somewhere in the dark of space there were other creatures like man, also scattering their seed from world to world. He envisaged the misfits and the outcasts hurled through the transfax to head-on collision with some alien race.

Frightened even by their own kind, suspicious of cleverness even in human shape, they would panic, they would fight.

And there were other consequences, too.

But you cannot hide knowledge. Somewhere, someone else would discover the technique of the transfax. It might not be soon, for he had stumbled across the relevant mathematics only because of a suspected error in other calculations; men were thinking in terms of crossing space in ships, not abolishing space between objects.

So he had put his trust in himself, and promised himself he would be worthy of it, and he had gone out to find others whom he could learn to trust.

During the initial period he had laid down principles which had later been observed religiously, such as that no one granted a fresh term of life through the transfax should be given back the identical body he or she had formerly possessed. It would have been too dangerous if someone known to have died in unquestioned circumstances were later to be seen alive and well and recognizable. Nor was the shape of one's new body left to the owner to decide; that was for others to choose, sympathetically, honestly, but without favor.

Then the sparks he struck began to set fires. He remembered as though it were a day of rebirth the time when he first recognized that he could trust another person with his knowledge — a person truly aware of the needs and shortcomings of mankind.

There were three thousand of them now, and more to come.

His feelings were strangely mixed, neither joy nor relief, but rather satisfaction. He had atoned in some way for his high-handedness in decreeing that such a thing should not be given to mankind at large. Doubtless thousands upon thousands had died who might have lived, and might have made their new term of life valuable to their race. But Counce felt now that, had they a chance to judge, they might forgive his arrogance in appointing himself arbiter of man's destiny.

Well, now there was Wu, and Katya, and Ram, and Falconetta, and Verity, and all the rest — and there was notably Anty Dreean, who might even be the person Counce could trust with the ultimate responsibility: the *whole* responsibility.

He was deadly tired, completely weary of bearing the burden he had carried for three long centuries, and he longed more than anything else to find oblivion.

CHAPTER XVI

AFTER THE FIRST two weeks or so, Enni Zatok had given up all attempts to resist, or even to think. Somewhere behind her drawn, pale face rebellion still smoldered, personality still existed. But outwardly she was like a mechanical toy, moving, occasionally speaking, no more.

There had been events she could not understand — without pain, but with infintely worse effects: shame, desecration of the privacy of her mind. They had studied her even to the darkest levels of her subconscious, till they had extracted every grain of knowledge she could give them. In old-fashioned terms, in Ymiran terms, they had taken her soul.

And still they were not satisfied.

The room in which she had lived during this period was white-walled, stark, hardly furnished. It was rather equipped than furnished, in fact — with computers on wheeled carriages, electroencephalographs, machines that hummed and pulsed and shone rhythmical series of light-flashes into her eyes until she found herself seized with uncontrollable fits. They had forced her to remember details of her past life; now they knew more than she did about it. They had stripped her unexpectedly to analyze her reaction to violation of her modesty; they had shouted at her to see her reflex of surprise. There seemed to be nothing left.

And still they were unsatisfied!

She sat passively on the examination couch, her eyes fixed on a man called Bassett who had come more and more frequently to watch what was happening. In some way he seemed to be responsible for what they had done to her; therefore when she looked at him a faint flicker of hate showed behind her eyes. It was the only thing that betrayed the survival of her mind.

"I've told you again and again," Gold was saying. "We can't get anything more out of the girl! There's nothing there to be got!"

"But we haven't got what we wanted," Bassett snapped.

"Then it isn't there to be had," Gold answered shortly. "I know what we're looking for well enough. If we'd had the faintest suspicion that it was there, we'd have dug for it. You'll simply have to face the facts, and that's all there is to it."

"Damnation!" Bassett began to stride up and down the room, glancing occasionally at Enni as she sat silent in her gown. "There *has* to be an answer!"

Gold passed a weary hand across his eyes. "If there is, there's no way of finding it. The girl can't tell us any more. If subjective experience of Ymiran society doesn't provide even a clue, we haven't a hope."

Bassett drove fist into palm, angrily, and took a deep breath. "Well, then — we'll call their bluff!"

Hating himself, hating what he was doing, he went back to his own office and sent for his secretary. "Get on to Advertising," he ordered her. "Find out what lines they're currently plugging. Then ring Video India and book air time for one of them on the Falconetta Show."

If his secretary was surprised, she was too well trained to show it. She merely nodded and went out. Half an hour later she reported that the job had been done; half an hour later again, Gold rang through in a wild and agitated voice.

"She's gone!" he exclaimed. "Out of a locked room with no windows — the Ymiran girl has gone!"

Bassett did not reply. He merely broke the connection and sat staring out of his window over the roofs of Rio. That fitted. Oh, yes, it all fitted together now. Doubtless they thought they had been very clever. But he was determined to prove they were no cleverer than he.

He went home early that evening, to his vast apartment by the sea. His personal servant informed him that there was a gentleman to see him, and it was without surprise that he found the same man waiting for him as had been sitting in a boat in mid-Pacific when he returned from Boreas.

"Good evening," said Counce equably. "Please sit down."

Bassett remained standing, looking down on the visitor. "You must be feeling very self-satisfied," he ground out. "I have to admit I admire your gall in putting down that Ymiran girl as bait."

Counce raised one eyebrow slightly. "How astute of you to realize," he said. "Belatedly, of course. However, you won't want to waste time on the past. It's the future that matters."

Breathing heavily, Bassett took a chair opposite the visitor. "All right," he said. "Either you ingeniously duped me when you maintained the solution to the problem lay on Ymir, or my staff is incompetent. Tell me which."

"Neither," said Counce, and leaned forward with his elbows on his thighs. "You'll forgive me if I don't go into details as to exactly why we are prepared to co-operate with you on your schemes, won't you? I am going to say no more than that, while our ends differ, our means here coincide.

"Your failure to see the solution you hunted for so desperately depended on two things: first, you did not recognize that emigrants from Earth are lazy, to put it bluntly, by outworld standards; and second, you were not thinking far enough back from your ultimate objective.

"Obviously, the government of a world like Boreas would sense the sting in the tail of a bargain involving acceptance of Earthborn immigrants in exchange for aid. Earthborn are demanding, influential, used to a very high standard of living, and what's worse, the colonial peoples regard them with acute jealousy. From that it's a short step to thinking of them as a threat.

"But if you were to ask them to accept industrious men and women from Ymir . . ."

Bassett could not help himself; he felt a smile spread unbidden across his face. "Of course you're right," he said at last. "No one regards Ymirans as a menace — only as rather foolish cranks. And it would breach the dam separating the parochial-minded outworlds."

"Please don't think you can now welsh on your agreement," Counce said in a stern voice, "and attempt to put this into practice by yourself. How are you intending to persuade Ymirans to leave their world? I can assure you that looking for the answer to that subordinate problem will cost you more heartache than you've already had."

Bassett looked at him. "I'll take your word on it," he said slowly. "How do *you* propose to set about it?"

"We have agents in Ymir," Counce answered obliquely. "All we need is the resources you can command. We will give you a fair chance to outwit us later, when our intentions again diverge; for the moment, all we ask is your assistance."

"In what shape?"

"I'll give you the full details later. I assure you the requirements will not amount to more than you originally intended to devote to the project. Manpower, money, technical equipment — but most of all, pure power. Do you consent?"

He could see the reservations Bassett was mentally making as clearly as though they were being written on the man's forehead. No matter; he had won.

Instead of passing the good news by the impersonal method of sending a written message through the transfax, he decided to make the trip to Regis himself, because he had another job to attend to at the same time. Before leaving, he checked with Falconetta.

"How is she?" he demanded; there was no need to explain whom he meant.

"Pitiable!" said Falconetta savagely. "There doesn't seem to be anything left of her — she's just a husk."

"Has Ram seen her?"

"No, unfortunately. He's up on the Video India satellite having fits about the stuff Bassett sent us to put on the show. You know he's always avoided buying air time with us, because we refuse to allow the use of hypnotics or subliminal suggestion. He wasn't missing a trick, though; it looks as if he decided to make the most of his compulsory expenditure. Ram says he's never seen such loaded stuff."

"It's probably a standard handout, issued by one of the department staff — not Bassett's personal choice."

"Did he give in?" Falconetta sounded as though she had only just remembered to ask.

"Yes, of course. I'm going to Regis now to tell Wu and start arranging things. But there's one thing I want to ask you to do if you can spare the time . . ."

The news spread to everyone on Regis within moments of Counce's arrival; everyone consequently took a few minutes off from work to crowd around and congratulate him. It was a considerable achievement to have made Bassett yield. But looking around the group, Counce noticed one person missing.

"Where's Anty?" he demanded, and there was a sudden silence.

"He's in pretty bad shape," said Katya after a pause. "We just don't seem able to get through to him. Last I saw he was outside the base sitting on a rock and looking at the desert."

"He got tired of that and went up to the polar base to look at some ice," Lotus Scharf contradicted with unusual cynicism.

"Excuse me, then," said Counce, and forced his way over to the transfax.

Just as Lotus had said, Anty was looking at some ice. There was hardly anything else to be seen at this polar base except the tent where Friend, the alien, was quartered. Anty was walking moodily up and down the edge of the excavation from which they had dug the proof of the Others' first visit, occasionally kicking a lump of frozen mud into the pit. He seemed to have adjusted perfectly to his new, slightly different body, and his movements were natural and free. But his hunched attitude oozed depression.

It was always a shock to Counce to see a friend changed, even when — as in Anty's case — he had helped with the work of altering the record to change the bodily appearance. It was delicate work, but they had never yet made an error; and if they did, there were always other, older records to base their new design on. Counce recalled himself sternly to his immediate purpose.

"Anty!" he said. The young man did not cease his aimless pacing; barely even showed that he had heard.

Counce walked over to him and fell in alongside. "I have a job for you, Anty," he said. "Rather an important one."

Anty gave him a sidelong sneer. The new face he had acquired was darker than his old one; long-nosed, sharp-jawed, it was rather a good-looking face. A lock of uncontrollable black hair showed beneath his hood. "You'd better give it to someone else," he snapped. "I couldn't organize a short walk."

"Are you still harping on the Others' behavior? What makes you think you're responsible for what they did?"

"I should have known," Anty responded moodily. "So should you, come to that."

"There's only one kind of incurable fool — the man who can't learn from experience," Counce said sharply. "You're busy building yourself a reputation as one. But you're not very good at it. If you don't trust yourself, I do. Come on, I'm taking you back to Main Base to set you to work."

Anty halted and stared at his companion as if he had never seen him before. At length he shrugged, and gave a reluctant nod.

There was a small group of people waiting for them beside the transfax when they emerged into the brilliant equatorial sunshine again. Among them was a girl, fair-haired, blue-eyed, who stood a little apart from the rest, taking no apparent interest in her surroundings.

"That's Enni Zatok," said Counce softly. "You know who she is, don't you? You know what she's gone through. Right now, she doesn't really think; she barely even reacts. But before Bassett got hold of her, Jaroslav said she was the best potential recruit he'd found on Ymir. I'm giving you the most responsible job you've ever had, Anty. I'm telling you to fetch her back out of the fog she's in and turn her into a valuable recruit. Don't say you can't do it. You can. You're going to."

Slowly, Anty was peeling off the protective clothing he had worn at the arctic base. Not saying a word, he got down from the transfax platform and went across to Enni, who gave him a blank, distrustful look. When he put out his hand tentatively, she shied away.

But after a moment, Anty smiled, and the faintest hint of a counterpart turned up the corners of Enni's mouth.

Counce gave a contented sigh, and walked away.

CHAPTER XVII

"AT A ROUGH GUESS," Counce had said thoughtfully, "it will take us four months to visit every world we intend sending Ymirans to — which is to say *every* world. That allows for traveling time."

Bassett had given him a cynical smile. He had come to accept Counce as a declared enemy turned temporary ally. The understanding between them was complete, if peculiar. He had said, "You could shorten that period considerably with your matter transmitter."

Counce had shaken his head in amusement. "For one thing," he lied straight-faced, "we haven't the power resources to use it regularly. For another, I've no doubt at all that you would then proceed to pack your entourage with technicians who would seize every chance of inspecting the machinery. You've got a Metchnikov driver in your private ship — that will be quite fast enough for our purposes."

So it was done.

There was no doubt that Bassett's reputation had spread since he achieved his position of influence on Earth; certainly the respect with which the Grand Lama of K'ung-fu-tse received his visitor was considerable.

"They are indeed said to be diligent and industrious on Ymir," the Grand Lama conceded. "From all accounts, they are compelled to be by the harsh nature of their world."

He glanced complacently at the pleasant expanse of greenery about him; he held audience in the open air, under a sacred tree imported from Earth, with two attendants fanning him.

"*But,*" he added, "they are also reported to be hard and intolerant. I doubt that they will harmonize with my people."

Smoothly, with considered reasoning, the visitors demolished his misgivings. They oiled the bargain with certain valuable technical consignments which were badly needed on K'ung-fu-tse. And when they departed, the Grand Lama congratulated Bassett on his desire to assist his fellow men.

The President of Boreas had had dealings with Bassett before, on a slightly different but essentially similar question. They got nothing better out of him than a promise of careful consideration, but they could tell from the avaricious look in his eyes that he would come around sooner or later.

After all, a third of a million Ymirans could be given some land nobody else would think fit for use, and what they did after that was their own affair.

"Why the devil do they want to leave Ymir?" snapped the Tyrant of Zeus. "Don't tell me," he added, holding up a carefully manicured hand. "This is a bunch that's finally gotten sick of living like fakirs between icebergs and mountains. A third of a million is a hell of a lot to wake up to sanity all at once, though."

"It seems to be a movement which has been growing for a considerable time," Bassett explained.

"Must have been! Well, what's your interest in the matter?"

Bassett gave a conspiratorial smile. "Three hundred thousand people who've decided that mortifying the flesh isn't such a good idea after all are going to want to buy a lot of worldly comforts," he explained. "A lot of them, of course, they'll buy on Zeus, but I'd venture to suggest that I could arrange imports, dutiable imports . . ."

The Tyrant gave an emphatic nod. This was his language. He called for paper and a pen to sign an agreement.

And so it went. At the end of four months they had organized homes on decent planets for all but half a million of the people of Ymir.

"The rest Earth can take, right?" Counce demanded of Bassett. The other shrugged.

"Probably. However, it seems to me that we've gone ahead rather rapidly. Do the Ymirans know yet that there are these new homes waiting for them?"

"Not yet," said Counce with a hint of grimness. "But I bet there are a lot of them who wish they were already off the planet . . ."

The next time the *Amsterdam* called on Ymir, Jaroslav was not at home. Puzzled, Captain Leeuwenhoek confronted the elders of Festerburg and demanded to know what had happened.

"No one knows," the elders assured him, desperately attempting to convey their sincerity. Leeuwenhoek looked them over contemptuously from his much greater height. *Runts,* he reflected.

"All right!" he snapped. "We warned you that if anything happened to Jaroslav Dubin, we'd be happy to forget about this icebox of a world. I call here out of charity more than anything else, and that goes for my colleagues too. Last time I was here, you were trying to frame Jaroslav on some charge involving a girl. I guess you realized we'd see through a fake like that one, but I should have thought experienced liars like you could come up with a better answer than a plain denial."

The elders exchanged cowed glances. In the holds of the *Amsterdam* was a supply of live sperm for their next season's cattle; bulls fed on the exiguous diet of Ymiran cattle-food were more often sterile than not. There was also cold-resistant wheat, which they badly needed.

But their protests were in vain, and in a towering rage Leeuwenhoek headed for space with his cargo still aboard. He knew plenty of other markets for what he carried. His parting shot was a promise never to come back.

Shaken, the elders called their custodians and set them to searching for Jaroslav Dubin. They had never expected to *want* to see the man. But the truth — the surprising truth — was that until Leeuwenhoek accused them of making away with Jaroslav Dubin, they had no inkling that he was not where he always was: in his sinfully luxurious home.

They turned Festerburg upside down; hunted his house from floor to roof. Even to discover his dead body would have meant that they could plead with the space traders. But they found nothing.

Jaroslav had vanished off the face of Ymir.

As one of the elders remarked, it looked as though the man had dug himself a hole, climbed in, and pulled the hole in after him. He had no idea how literally exact that was. Jaroslav had climbed through his transfax, and had pulled that off Ymir when he had used it, so the parallel was in fact precise. But all the puzzled searchers found was an empty cavity leading nowhere.

Their puzzlement turning rapidly to apprehension, they awaited the visit of the next spaceship, and this time got their disclaimers in first. The captain of the ship was as adamant in disbelieving them as Leeuwenhoek had been, and he too departed without unloading, swearing he would not be back.

"They cannot all say the same!" the more optimistic elders declared.

But they did. And within two months the specter of famine hung gaunt and ghastly across the face of Ymir.

In vain the elders tried to argue that it was a gift from heaven, enabling the weak-willed to fulfill the original aims of the founding fathers. That line cut no ice with parents whose ears were sore with the continual crying of hungry children; with mothers who could not feed their newborn babies; with adults whose conversation was always being interrupted by the grumbling of their unfilled bellies.

The most indignant of all the population were the young people — those between childhood and maturity. Now the fruits of Jaroslav's campaign of subversion became plain to the appalled elders. Boys and girls whom everyone had believed well-behaved and strictly moral openly admitted that they had been friendly with Jaroslav and that they believed he was right and the elders wrong. Moreover they began openly to accuse the elders of having done away with Jaroslav and thus of having brought this terrible situation about.

Then the visits from spaceships stopped altogether. The word must have gone around. And the Ymirans realized that they were totally isolated and completely helpless, for they were too poor as a planet ever to have acquired even a single spaceship of their own. They had no means of getting a message to another inhabited planet except at the tardy velocity of light; long before an SOS had been received, they would have starved to death.

Even the elders, faced with this prospect, were unable to maintain that they wanted to reap the rewards of righteousness forthwith.

Now the long-pent hatreds began to burst forth. Parents could no longer cow their children; gangs of young people began to roam the streets, stoning the houses of the elders and jumping any custodians who ventured to interfere. "If they're going to starve us to death, we might as well get back at them first!" they maintained, and proceeded to beat the custodians savagely with their own night sticks.

But their cries grew weaker as hunger grew stronger.

Those who had thought to hoard a little extra food, and were unwise enough not to be careful about pretending to be hungry when among strangers, found their stocks rifled; sometimes they were publicly execrated or spattered with filth. And then there came the day when a half-beaten child's body was found on the street . . .

"Never again will an Ymiran be able to pretend he is any better than another man," said Counce, stony-faced. He raised his eyes to meet Bassett's. "I think we can now begin."

Bassett nodded. The spaceship in which he and Counce were traveling was only one of a huge fleet circling Ymir — these were the kind of resources Counce had chiefly needed to implement his careful plan. Ships and men. And power.

Now, at Bassett's command, the ships broached air and made towards their landing points. The most expert pilots to be found had been enlisted for this task; only a fortunate few would be able to set down at the regular port in Festerburg, and the rest would have to make do with what flat ground they could find.

To the frightened people of Ymir, the arrival of the ships was like a miracle. When they had been sure they would die out, unknown, they found life promised them anew. Their directionless anger subsided; they looked again to their elders, and it was a quiet crowd that surrounded the first of the ships to put down.

Counce went down with the group headed for Festerburg, since it was the capital of the planet. He had half expected the ships to be stormed by a mob demanding to be fed; as it turned out, the Ymirans seemed unable to convince themselves the ships were really there, and did not want to risk destroying the illusion.

He came out of the lock of the ship which had brought him and found a group of elders, drawn of face, drab of dress, waiting a few paces ahead of the silent crowd of watchers. He looked down on them thoughtfully.

"We have brought food," he said, and an amplifier carried his words to every corner of the crowd. A ragged, half-hearted cheer broke out, died swiftly.

"We have not brought much, and we shall bring no more," Counce asserted. "We — all men — have better things to do than to give charity to fools."

A slow grumbling sound; it, like the cheer, died swiftly.

"Yes, you're fools! With a score or more pleasant worlds to choose from, planets on which men can live like men instead of like burrowing animals, your ancestors condemned you to dependence on the charity of others. Because this world is not fit for human beings to live on!"

A boy of eighteen in the front rank of the crowd jumped forward a yard and shook his fist at the small group of elders. "It's the truth!" he screamed.

"You've had long enough to play at being a chosen people," said Counce. Now he was looking straight down at the elders again, and they were shuffling their feet on the cold ground. "I think the last few weeks have taught you that you are proud, stupid, and stiff-necked. But all your pride was not proof against the complaining of your bellies."

The elders did not reply.

"So we are going to give you a last chance," Counce concluded. "Because we do not think that anyone who acts differently from ourselves is necessarily an enemy, we have gone to much trouble and much difficulty, first, to bring you food enough to keep you alive for a day or two, and secondly, to arrange homes for you on decent planets with decent climates. I'm giving you a choice now; stay and starve, or leave Ymir."

He waited. But not for long.

After that, although a few fanatics maintained it was better to stay and starve, there was negligible opposition, and the ships opened their holds and discharged their cargoes. The fanatics warned those who accepted the food that they were selling their souls; the answers they got revealed that despite the rigors of Ymiran discipline a surprisingly complete vocabulary of abuse had survived.

But the spaceships did not only carry food, part of their cargo consisted of knocked-down spaceships, hulls. With drivers, emergency rations, and oxygen-generators, they could shift Ymirans by the thousand, cramped, still hungry, but hopeful.

As the reports came in from the four other cities on the planet, and revealed that the situation in all of them was the same, Bassett glanced at Counce.

"Your agents on Ymir seem to have been remarkably efficient," he said, drawing his eyebrows together. "I'd never have credited that such a response could be obtained from Ymirans."

Counce answered dryly, "Maybe you didn't give sufficient credit to the power of the basic instincts. They don't have hungry men on Earth these days, do they?"

Bassett fell silent again; his eyes seemed to be looking into the future. Doubtless he still imagined he would be able to carry his schemes to fruition; doubtless he was picturing the future in which he would be the acknowledged unifier of the human race.

Fortunately for the human race — and for the Others — he was imagining the wrong future.

CHAPTER XVIII

"I DON'T UNDERSTAND," said Lecoq savagely. "There hasn't been *any* trouble! These Ymirans have just been swallowed up on every world we've taken them to — gone as meekly as lambs to the slaughter. Only there hasn't been any slaughter."

"There's no clue to where this man Counce went, I suppose," Bassett said meditatively. He made it a statement, not a question.

Outside, a dull afternoon had blurred the view of Rio; it matched the mood he was in perfectly.

So these mysterious people had fulfilled their promise; everything had gone as they had said it would — Ymir evacuated, its people accepted, tolerated, laughed at here and there for their peculiar ways of speech and behavior, but without real problems. The dam had been breached. Now, if the possibilities were carefully developed, there could again be a flow of people from world to world. . . .

He grew aware that Lecoq was answering him. "Not a sign," he was saying in disgusted tones. "We kept as close a watch on him as we possibly could during the whole operation, trying to find some clue to relate him to others of his group; there was nothing. Then, at the end, he just vanished when my man's back was turned. I dismissed the man, of course, but it probably wasn't altogether his fault."

"Well, two things are clear," Bassett said abruptly. "We can't tolerate a powerful secret society like this — we need that matter transmitter of theirs, for one thing — and what's more, we can't continue to let them use us."

Lecoq's eyes held puzzlement. He said, "I can't make out what it is they want. They seem to have done everything *we* wanted."

"But not for the same reasons, that's definite. Did we manage to identify anyone who could perhaps be an associate of Counce's?"

"Several people who *could* be." Lecoq opened a bulky folder on his knee and selected documents from it. "Almost beyond a doubt, this Ymiran, Jaroslav Dubin; unfortunately he could be anywhere in the galaxy right now. We're looking for him. His disappearance was too neat, too patly timed, to have been coincidental. And look at the consequences."

"But we can't rule out the possibility that he was merely kidnapped by Counce's group," Bassett remarked heavily. "And who else?"

"Probably someone on the staff of Video India. I've investigated the people involved in the Falconetta Show, and there are half a dozen of them who disappear unaccountably for short periods. Falconetta herself is one."

Bassett raised his eyebrows. "Really! It doesn't surprise me, I must say. How about this old man who produces the show — the one who's been complaining to our advertising department about the copy we sent them?"

"Him too. And then there are individuals on all the outworlds who may conceivably be connected with Counce. They turned up on the spot when we delivered the

Ymirans, took charge, and walked off again when things were straightened out. We haven't been able to establish that any of them arrived or departed by matter transmitter, though. They're all respected and influential local citizens-civil servants, scientists, doctors, psychologists — but none of them would have been expected to make himself responsible for a group of immigrants without some special reason."

Bassett nodded, his eyes skimming rapidly down the pages of the reports. "There's a sort of picture emerging," he said. "The impression I get is of a long-established undercover organization which recruits its members very carefully and offers them advantages such as the matter transmitter in return for unquestioning obedience. It's the scope of the things they can offer which makes our job so difficult. I doubt whether we could easily buy one of them, even if we managed to identify him beyond doubt."

"There's a warning in the way they managed to get the Ymiran girl away from us, too," said Lecoq mournfully. "I suspect they keep a careful watch on all their members, and if one of them is unaccounted for, they take steps to make certain he isn't selling the organization out."

"We must have the matter transmitter," Bassett said flatly. "I doubt whether this group could have been set up in the first place without it. Why hasn't someone else invented it by now?"

"Maybe they are so well organized they can find out whenever there's a risk of that happening," Lecoq suggested. "And they buy the inventor off, or silence him."

Bassett shook his head. "They'd need to be hellishly efficient to do that without any news leaking out at all. I don't want to give them credit for more than is reasonable.

By the way, how many people have you involved directly in this? I mean, how many people besides ourselves know now about the existence of Counce's group?"

"So far as the staff of the company is concerned, and all the other people who were involved in the evacuation of Ymir, it doesn't exist. I can say that quite definitely. The idea of evacuating Ymir was yours, and I put it into practice. I think it would be bad for morale if we let it be known that we were acting under—well, under blackmail."

"Agreed." Bassett thumbed through the papers Lecoq had given him. "Well, what we must do now is obvious. We must investigate the most likely of these people whose names are on the list, and somehow get the facts from them."

"Starting with Video India?" Lecoq suggested. Bassett inclined his head.

Counce had in fact stepped back across the parsecs to Regis as soon as he judged the remainder of the evacuation could be left to Bassett's capable staff. There was much to be done — with Friend, the alien survivor; with Enni Zatok; with Anty Dreean. Besides, it was absolutely certain that Bassett would not rest content with what he had. Sooner or later he was going to find the existence of their group intolerable, and seek a way of attacking it.

He had been congratulating Anty on the way in which he had restored Enni's self-confidence and alert brightness — admitting only to himself, for it was a cynical thought, that a fundamental question of human nature had done more than Anty's actual help. He was standing with the young man alongside the transfax platform, watching the Ymiran girl, who lay in the sunlight fifty yards distant, eyes closed. She wore nothing but dark glasses, and her pale, sun-starved skin had tanned to golden brown.

It was the measure of a considerable achievement, to have rid her of her deep-seated irrational conditioning about clothes. Counce had said so.

"It's like everything else. An individual who is at the mercy of a reaction not based on necessity is that much a malfunctioning person. Take our attitude towards the Others, for instance."

Anty blinked. "I don't see the connection."

"No? Think it over. When they came out fighting from their ship, they were motivated by such a reaction. We, by contrast, were acting strictly from logical necessity. The chance of hostile contact between our races is a disaster; we're free to maintain that our efforts to promote peaceful understanding are idealistic and all that, but when you reduce it to essentials, it's the necessity of saving our own skins, not the hope of some future benefit for both our races, which really drives us on."

"I'm with you," Anty nodded.

Counce gave him a sidelong glance. He really was quite handsome in his new body. A stir of envy rose in Counce's mind, and subsided again at once.

"Pretty, isn't she?" he said casually.

"Who, Enni? Yes, she is," Anty answered with an unsuccessful attempt at equal casualness, and Counce gave him a grin before turning away.

As he passed the door of Wu's office, the door was flung back and the director hailed him. "News from Ram, Saïd!" he called. "Bassett's put two and two together."

"Has he now!" Counce went into the cool shadow of the office; Wu had four fans going so hard they were almost blowing the files off his desk.

"It can't be coincidence that four of his firm's staff have been making casual inquiries about where Ram, Falconetta and our other two agents spend their off-duty time." Wu kept his eyes on Counce's face, watching for his reaction.

"That's the other two at Video India, you mean," Counce said with irritating obtuseness. Wu took a deep breath and nodded.

"What do you recommend we should do about it?"

"Why, tell them, of course." Counce didn't blink or smile.

"*Tell* them? You're out of your mind!"

"Not at all. We knew we had to come at least partly into the open to impress Bassett and enlist his help. If he's been a little quicker than we anticipated in picking up the unavoidable clues we left, we can't help that." Counce took a chair, swung it round, and sat down facing Wu across the back of it.

"Now as I see it, the problem is perfectly simple. So long as Bassett gets enough information about us to keep him happy, there's small risk of him finding out something about us that we don't know he knows. I want you to tell Ram to supply Bassett with enough data to lead him to Regis."

"What for?"

"I want Bassett out here, on his own. Where we can deal with him on our terms." Counce's eyes seemed to cloud over, as though he were looking at a memory. "It seems to me, Wu — without wishing to be conceited — that in essence there are two human beings. Archetypes, if you like. I'm one. Bassett is the other.

"Do you know, I was just about his age when I stumbled across the transfax? Bassett is brilliant. So was I, in a different field. But we think differently. We both plan, take thought for the consequences of our actions, but our motives are parsecs apart."

Wu sat down silently. He had a feeling that he was not

really meant to be listening, that Counce's soliloquy was for himself alone.

"Maybe if Bassett had been in the same situation as I was, if he'd seen he had the chance of not just one lifetime, but many lifetimes, to work out his plans, he would have done as I did. But I can't really believe that. He wouldn't have given a damn for the fact that the Ymirans were living under conditions unfit for any decent person, if it hadn't happened to provide him with a means of implementing his plans for himself."

He roused himself and stood up. "Ram will be able to fix things," he said briskly. "I want Bassett here, in his private ship, not knowing quite what he expects to find. And I'll handle him after that."

Wu nodded.

"Meantime," Counce continued, "I'm going to step up to the polar base and check on how Friend is getting on. I have a sneaking suspicion we may have been wrong about him."

Wu looked slightly alarmed. "How?"

"Well, Falconetta seems to have made such strides in gaining his confidence, I'm inclined to think we could scrap our plans for preventing contact with the Others, and merely limit it. After all, Ymir stands empty now, waiting for them. Why should we not give it to them at once, as proof of our good intentions? So long as we make it perfectly plain that the gift is conditional on their not infringing human-occupied space elsewhere, I think we could safely intermingle with them — even invite them to maintain a base on Regis, perhaps. We dictate the circumstances, naturally. But the information this will give us about their psychology and their emotional attitudes would more than make up for the trouble of undertaking all the contact work ourselves."

"That seems reasonable," nodded Wu. "In fact," he added, enthusiasm mounting, "it sounds thoroughly attractive. How soon would you want to do it?"

"At once," said Counce, and went out.

CHAPTER XIX

FRIEND had taken things into his own —not exactly hands, but they served the same purpose. Now, when Counce stepped from the transfax into the frigid northern air, he could see at once the slight but unmistakable impact of alien thought-patterns on his surroundings. There was a building, to begin with, proportioned differently from human dwelling. It was not much more than a hut, but expertly made out of blocks of permafrozen soil, sealed with ice which glistened under the stars. There was a sort of garden before it — colored rocks and stones, low-growing alien plants of grayish-green which must have come from seeds included as food in the cargo of the alien ship.

He went direct to the entrance of the hut, and that too was inhumanly planned, proportioned to a blocky, thick-set alien body. He knocked at the door and was invited in by Falconetta.

There was nothing much in the room, except the couch they had taken from the ship, shelves to serve as tables and things which Friend had asked to have made or had made for himself. Falconetta, wrapped in her furs because the air inside the hut was no warmer than that outside, squatted on a cushion on the floor; Friend himself was on the couch. Between them there was a finished version of the language converter the technicians had designed when Friend arrived.

"Why, Saïd!" Falconetta exclaimed in delight. "How good to see you. Friend, this is —"

The language converter grunted and interrupted itself; it was disconcerting to hear the alien version of the words at the same time as the human, but doubtless one got used to that, Counce reflected. Certainly Falconetta did not seem put out.

"I remember you," Friend said; they had given him a deep, rather pleasantly masculine voice by setting the controls appropriately. "You were the one who untied me when I was first here. I never thanked you. I was afraid then, but not any more."

Counce felt a surge of satisfaction. He smiled at the alien, wondering if he had learned to interpret this offensive gesture of displaying one's fangs as it was meant to be interpreted.

"I don't know if anyone told you," Falconetta said, "but I discovered that Friend studied ecology, and was on this flight as a trainee expert in colonial settlement. Their disciplines appear to have a lot in common with ours."

"And in ecological terms," Friend qualified, "it now appears perfectly plain to me that the galaxy will contain us both to our mutual benefit. This is strange, but I know it."

"I think," said Counce reflectively, "that I should like to show you something and ask your opinion as an ecologist about it. Falconetta, have you time to spare? Are you not needed back on Earth?"

"I went back the day before yesterday and arranged with Ram to use up some shows we have in the can already," she replied. "I'm free for some time to come now." Dryly, she added, "So far as education goes, I think I'm doing a good job here."

"I don't think you need worry about depending too much on physical attraction," Counce grunted, glancing at the alien's gray hide and wondering by what standards he judged the females of his own species. That would have been a problem if they'd decided to keep Friend isolated from his own people for a long time; it was reasonable to assume that a young functioning male had the same sort of psychological difficulties among the Others.

Friend naturally missed the implications of the remark, and his heavy head switched in puzzlement from side to side, but he made no comment.

"Right," said Counce, making the decision. "Come with me."

It wasn't too much of a risk, bringing Friend to Ymir by transfax. Chances were, the alien had already figured out that mankind had such a device anyway; how else would they have snatched a full-sized ship from its course?

Ymir was not quite barren, of course; there were the empty cities to bear witness to human occupation, and the fields of hardy winter-bearing wheat, and the starving cattle that had had to be left behind in the evacuation. But aside from that, and the indigenous life, it was empty. Waiting.

To save power, Counce sent forward a transfax unit first; he chose a spot for it where a cross section of the whole planet would spring into view — ice-ridged mountains, bare, rocky plains, an inlet of the floe-scattered sea, rolling yellowish-gray against the shore.

They stepped through one after the other: Counce first, then Friend, apprehensively, but bravely, and Falconetta last. The two humans stood shivering in a blast even icier than that of Regis' polar regions, but the alien stepped forward almost reverently.

While he was surveying the scene, Counce caught Falconetta's eye and grinned; she gave an answering nod and a smile. The language converter, which had been refined to lightness and ease of carrying, stood beside her. Counce picked it up and directed it towards Friend.

"This is the world you surveyed from space on your last trip," he said, and Friend swung round in altogether human astonishment.

"But that's not possible," the converter boomed. "We saw that it was populated by your kind."

Counce thought of the things that had happened since then. Time enough for detailed explanations later; for now, let it appear a truly disinterested action. He said, choosing his words carefully, "We did not need this planet. Some of us had come here to live, but it was hard for them to find enough to eat. Therefore when we discovered that your race favored such worlds as this, we concluded you would be able to make better use of it. Could you?"

"*Could* we?" Friend threw up his forelimbs to embrace the landscape. "Why, this is the most beautiful world I ever saw!"

Counce drew his eyebrows together with a wry expression; he hoped Friend was far enough away for the look to be lost on him. But Falconetta saw it, and chuckled.

Friend was setting off on a tour of inspection; despite their coldness, they followed him, and it was more than two hours before they circled back towards the transfax through which they had come. They were barely within sight when they saw that someone stood on its platform, scanning the landscape.

"Excuse me," said Counce. "Someone wants us." He began to run, and as he came closer saw that the new arrival was Katya.

"So there you are!" she snapped. "I wish you'd been kind enough to let us know where you were going. It wasn't till we found Friend and Falconetta had both disappeared too that Wu had an inspiration. Damn it, we've got people looking for you over half the galaxy!"

Counce glanced round. "We've been enjoying ourselves," he murmured. "What's the trouble?"

"Only another alien ship headed for Ymir, that's all! We were getting set to drag it off its course when Wu said something about you having second thoughts, and we're going out of our minds with worry."

"How long will it be before it gets here?"

"Two to three days. We've got eight hours to seize it with the transfax before it gets out of range."

"Two to three days," echoed Counce thoughtfully. "All right, we'll let it come all the way, and when it arrives, we'll surprise them with a small reception committee. Regis Main," he said to the transfax robot, and stepped out of earshot before Katya could reply.

Counce would have given much to be a telepath when the ship swooped to its landing and the Others found one of their own kind waiting on the strange new world. He would have liked so much to know — instead of merely guessing — what the astonished reactions were. Still, the mere appearance was reward in itself.

Together, separately, they had talked to Friend during the intervening hours, pleading with him, impressing on him how much would stand or fall by his actions. But half of the work had already been done, and they felt very confident as they waited out of sight among the rocks surrounding the deserted spaceport. Friend alone stood in plain sight, with a hand amplifier hurriedly adapted to his peculiar form of grasp.

Officers came out first, their gray hides painted with many symbols of authority, and suspiciously surrounded the unexpected Friend. They carried guns; they glanced about them as if expecting attack, or a trap.

Friend spoke at length; he took them and showed them the neighborhood — the empty town which had once been called Festerburg, the dying crops, the abandoned cattle. Then he brought them back to where they had started, and turned, and waved for someone to show himself.

Together, from opposite sides of the edge of the spaceport, Counce and Falconetta rose into view and walked unhurriedly towards the newcomers.

At a reasonable distance they stopped, and Falconetta raised the language converter she carried. Friend had told them what was best to say; she recited it carefully, a traditional formula of friendship among the Others.

Puzzled, but beginning to believe, they set their guns aside, and one of them — the ship's captain, presumably— approached the two humans. He looked them up and down. At length he indicated the language converter.

It was confusing to hear the same voice as Friend's come from the machine when the new speaker made inquiry, but of course that was the only voice the device was set for. It interpreted that the alien was asking how they had spoken in his language.

They told him. Friend confirmed what they said, and began to fill in the details.

"We are sorry for what happened to the crew of your first ship," Counce interrupted. "But they attacked us when we meant them no harm, and killed eighteen before we were forced to retaliate." He saw no point in mentioning that the eighteen deaths had cost nothing more than time, inconvenience and the expenditure of quantities of power on duplicating the casualties. "It will not, of course, happen again."

How ill-equipped they were for understanding each other, he reflected. These explanations, this fumbling towards a sort of mutual trust. . . . He took a deep breath and said, "I think you are afraid of us. If you are very much afraid, you may go away. Do not ever come back. But if you think you can learn not to be afraid, we will give you this planet for your people."

He waited for the big gray alien to make up his mind how to answer; in the seconds that ticked past, he found himself suddenly feeling overwhelmed. At the task he had undertaken; at the efforts he had invested in planning for this moment. But most of all, at the power he wielded.

Surprise and awe filled his mind. *Here I am, he thought, one man, and I'm giving away a world, arbiter of the fate of my own race and another. There has never been a man with so much power.*

The alien captain had conferred with his officers, too low for the language converter to catch the words. Now he came back.

"We are not afraid," he said. "To prove that, we will give you our weapons."

Counce shrugged. "If you like," he said impressively. "They cannot do us any harm, in any case."

Now the others were coming forward, a little hesitantly; the aliens fell back to a tight group again. But there was no further need to worry; this problem too had at last been solved. Which meant that only one remained.

"Saïd!" Wu was whispering as he came close. "Saïd, there was just news from Earth. Bassett has caught on. Ram said he sent for his spaceship yesterday and hasn't been heard of since. He's probably coming to Regis. Are you sure you know what you're doing?"

Counce gave a ghost of a smile. "As sure as I ever am," he said wryly. "But wish me luck . . ."

CHAPTER XX

IT WAS AS IF THE achievement on Ymir had sapped his virtue; he was weary, not with physical fatigue, but with something that went much deeper. He had aged in the mind. Each time he had died, he had inherited a younger body than he had left, and the skills of the technicians who doctored the records prior to producing the duplicates made short work of the effects of senility. But the brain itself, the patterns of thought and memory, the personality, had to go on. And it was there that the effect of three centuries of unrelieved struggle for what he believed to be the best had left its mark.

He was alone at the Regis base. They had needed everyone they could muster on Ymir, just in case something went wrong. Robots kept watch, recorded happenings for later analysis. They were watching him, but they could not question or interfere, and that was all he wanted.

In a strange way, he felt almost ashamed of what he proposed to do — as though he was taking a coward's way out. And yet there was no one else he could depute the task to; he felt that the archetype of which he had spoken to Wu had taken possession of him, and he was no longer acting as a private person but as a force, driven by something vast and implacable.

He knew the transfax better than any other man in the galaxy, of course. Probably no one would be able to duplicate what he was doing, but just in case someone misguidedly thought to take a hand after he had gone, he took the time to plant half a dozen misleading clues. He had to hurry. Soon someone on Ymir would realize he had gone, and come to Regis as the obvious first choice among places where he might be found. It was imperative he should not be found.

At long last, his work was done. Delicate adjustments; extrapolation of data from the faint ripple of a spaceship wake, converted into variable settings on a transfax robot; power controlled within limits that over parsec-long distances might have seemed incredible.

He looked one last time around Regis and walked into the transfax field.

At first he did not quite believe that he had succeeded so perfectly. To place himself within an inch inside the hull of a ship traveling many times faster than light more than a parsec away — that was hard to credit. But he had managed it, and now he stood, staring down at the chess-game buried in the transparent table, aboard Bassett's ship.

There was no one in the room at the moment, but there were sounds of movement. Sooner or later Bassett would return. There was practically nowhere for him to go in a ship this size. Counce smiled, and went around behind the table to sit in Bassett's chair and help himself to one of Bassett's cigarillos. He could enjoy waiting.

Only an inch of the cigarillo had burned when the door slid back and Bassett came in. His mind was too shaken for him to recognize his visitor for a moment, and his face went white. He had to clutch at the edge of the table for support; he was quite incapable of speaking.

"Sit down, Bassett," said Counce softly. "I want to talk to you."

Bassett looked about him wildly. But the door had closed automatically behind him, and probably Lecoq was not listening this time, as he had been when they first faced each other in this same room. Numbly, as though afraid Counce might have other powers than his mere physical presence, he obeyed.

Counce waited till Bassett's breathing had resumed its normal tempo, and his face had flushed back towards its usual color. Then he tapped the ash from the cigarillo and looked him straight in the face.

"You were quite right about Ram Singh being one of our agents," he said quietly. "But you were quite wrong to believe that you had been clever in establishing that we have our base on a world which is unknown to the public at large. I told Ram to give you hints suggesting that was the case. I even told him to make sure you went to investigate in person, although I was fairly positive you wouldn't trust anyone else to do the job. It's hard to trust people completely."

"You — what do you want now?" said Bassett thickly.

"To stop you from doing what you want, of course." Counce leaned forward with one elbow on the transparent table. "You are a very dangerous man. Shall I tell you why?"

Bassett licked his lips; he was recovering his self-possession, and looking about him for a means of giving an alarm. He nodded, without interest, merely to gain time.

"Because although you're intelligent enough in most ways, you sometimes overlook the most obvious things. And you're powerful enough for your mistakes to be disastrous — not to yourself, perhaps, but to mankind at large."

Bassett's pride was wounded; he snapped, "How? What do you mean?"

"I told you on the occasion of our first meeting that you wanted to rule the galaxy. You overlooked something. You are not fit to rule the galaxy. We are. The proof is that we *already do*."

"I dispute that," Bassett countered. "You're a hole-and-corner secret society, with influence, perhaps, but no power."

"No power?" Counce's lip curled. "Is it not power to give away a planet as a gift? Is it not power to determine the fate of two races, to say that they shall exist in peace, not in war?"

"Two — did you say *two* races?" echoed Bassett. Counce nodded.

"Now you see the extent to which you are a dangerous man. You are an enemy of mankind, because your only friend is yourself."

"You're a liar and a fool," said Bassett with sudden calm. "Once before I called a bluff you put up. I'm doing it again. I have nothing to lose."

"True," nodded Counce. "You have already forfeited your right to life."

Bassett threw back his head. "Lecoq!" he shouted.

Counce got up from his chair. He eyes roved over the walls of the cabin, seeking the line which had earlier betrayed to him the removal of one of the bulkheads. Yes, there were the ends of the stress-compensators, without which the strain of the hyperphotonic drive would tear the ship apart.

He felt in his pocket for the only tool he would need — an ordinary knife.

There were sounds of running footsteps now, and the door was flung back. But Counce had already driven the blade of the knife into the narrow crack surrounding the first of the stress-compensators, and with a sharp sideways thrust had broken it loose.

"Stop him!" wailed Bassett. "He'll kill us all!"

The second time, the knife broke off as the compensator was wrenched from its place. But that was enough. Already there was the ominous noise of harmonics building up in the metal of the hull, making the plates bend and vibrate and shudder.

The certainty of death was in the faces of the men who had crowded into the room. But in Bassett's face there was growing surprise, and a kind of triumph, as he saw that Counce was making no attempt to escape.

When the hull-plates shook themselves to pieces a moment later, and brought Counce the oblivion he had so long craved, Bassett carried with him into death the certainty that his opponent was still there.

Cold . . .

And pain. Only there should have been nothing. Nothing at all except continued oblivion. This person called Saïd Counce should not have felt cold, or pain, or anything ever again.

He considered for a moment that they were resuscitating him from a recording. But that was ridiculous. He had been duplicated five times, and it was an almost instantaneous process. They had no business to be doing it anyway.

Then he discarded the idea altogether. For he remembered the space ship shivering to pieces around him, and there was certainly no recording of that memory in existence. He had not been through a transfax between then and his death, because that *was* his death.

Hadn't he made it clear enough to them that he was tired of life?

A burst of feeble, ridiculous anger filled him — ridiculous because he could not do anything about it. He could not move a muscle. Except, he suddenly discovered, his eyelids. They responded when he lifted them.

And there was a small face framed by fair hair. Blue eyes looked down at him.

He said questioningly, "Enni Zatok?"

"Why, we — we managed it!" Her voice was tremulous, and suddenly the blue eyes filled with tears. "Anty! Anty, he knew my name!"

The face with the blue eyes drew aside, to be replaced by a darker one, masculine this time. "Well, that's a miracle," a voice was saying.

Counce found the effort of keeping his eyes open exhausting. He retreated into darkness. "What on earth are you up to?" he said.

"Why, we've been looking for you for nearly a hundred years," said Enni. "One of the Others' ships found you and brought you back to Regis. You were quick-frozen in space when Bassett's ship blew up. We didn't know where you could possibly be at first, but then we thought that was probably the answer. And it was!" she finished triumphantly.

Counce opened one eye and looked at her. "A hundred years," he said thoughtfully. "You haven't changed much, have you?"

"Nor have you," said Anty happily. "Everyone else was determined to duplicate your last recording when we couldn't track you down, but I told them no, if you'd blown yourself up with Bassett, you had a damned good reason for doing it."

"How well you understand me," Counce said acidly. "Now I suppose you're going to build me up till I'm strong enough to cut my throat."

Enni drew in her breath sharply, horrified. "Do you mean that?" she whispered. "Or are you angry because I gave you an adrenalin shot a moment ago?"

Counce was silent for a while. Then he licked his lips and whispered, "Tell me what's happened in the past century. Maybe, if you've been doing well, I'll want to come back." He paused. "Who runs things now?"

"Anty, mostly," said Enni, with quiet pride in her man.

Behind Counce's closed eyes pictures began to form. The things that might have happened in a hundred years. That was a long enough rest, surely.

"All right," he said "I'll come back."